Colonel Blood
Romance and
Adventure . . .

The Romance & Adventures

of the notorious

COLONEL BLOOD

who attempted to steal

The Crown Jewels

FROM

The Tower of London

IN THE REIGN OF CHARLES II.

BY

Whittenbury Kaye

Fredonia Books
Amsterdam, The Netherlands

The Romance & Adventures of the Notorious
Colonel Blood

by
Whittenbury Kaye

ISBN: 1-58963-598-1

Fredonia Books
Amsterdam, The Netherlands
http://www.fredoniabooks.com

Part i.

THE ROMANCE

Part ii.

THE ADVENTURES

PREFACE

A few years ago the writer found the entry in the Newchurch Parish Registers of the marriage of the notorious Colonel Blood with Maria Holcroft, daughter of Colonel Holcroft, of Holcroft ; and being interested in the two characters he began to gather from all sources what information he could about them and their families, and this volume is the result of that search.

He does not lay claim to any originality in relating the Adventures, for most of them will be found in other works, but he does to the Romance, which is purely imaginary, founded upon the fact of the wedding having actually taken place on June 21st, 1650.

It was absolutely impossible to write the life of this notorious desperado without

Preface.

entering into the political history of the nation. The writer has, therefore, tried to draw a true picture of the political situation of the Country from 1648 right on into the restoration as far as 1680 ; and he has been greatly helped by consulting the works of Gardiner, Bright, Baines, Beaumont, etc.

E. W. W. K.

Newchurch Rectory
Culcheth
Warrington
May, 1903

viii.

AN

ELEGIE
ON CORONEL BLOOD

Notorious for stealing the Crown, etc.,
Who dyed the twenty-sixth of August, 1680.

———

THANK ye kind Fates for your last favour shown
    Of stealing BLOOD who lately stole the crown
We'll not exclaim so much against you since ;
As well as BEDLOE you have fetcht him hence,
He who hath been a plague to all mankind :
And never was to anyone a friend,
Nay to himself such torment was at last,
He wisht his life had long ago been past.
For who can bear a discontented minde.
Or any peace with an ill Conscience finde,
Thro' his whole Life, he practis'd Villany
And lov'd it though he nothing got thereby ;
At first uneasy at the King's return
With Secret malice his bold heart did burn,
Against his Sovereign, and on pretence
He had much wrong'd his feign'd Innocence ;

ix.

To IRELAND went, and several ways did try
Rather than he would unrevenged Dye,
To vent his malice on his MAJESTY—
But finding there all his attempts prove vain
To ENGLAND forthwith he returns again
And after some small time he had lived here
The first great thing in which he did appear,
Was rescuing from Justice CAPTAIN MASON
Whom all the WORLD doth know, t' have been a base one
The next ill Thing he Boldly undertook
Was barbarously seizing of a DUKE
Whom as he since confess'd, he did intend
To Hang for Injuries he did pretend
The DUKE had done him, though the World does know
His Grace was ne'er to a Good Man a Foe ;
Having through all, his many well spent Days
Serv'd his King and Country, several ways
And Patiently his troubles underwent
Finding a sweetness, ev'n in Banishment
And Death he Patiently wou'd have endur'd
The KING'S restoring could he have secur'd ;
A DUKE who being by Providence preserv'd,
Hath begot sons ; who valiantly have served
His MAJESTY, and great Renown Obtain'd
In many Battles by your valour gain'd,
Great OSSERY, who by his conduct wise
Did oft by stratagems his Foes surprize
And hath as often beat them with his sword,

Was the Eldest Son, of this most Noble LORD.
  But I my HEROE almost had forgot
And th' next thing he Engaged in was a PLOT
To seize the CROWN; and without doubt he who
So Great a Piece of Villany would do,
When he saw Time, wou'd have attempted too;
His MAJESTY; but failing of the prize,
About the Town he undiscover'd lies,
Harbour'd by some of 's fellow Rogues, but see
How few can scape concerned in Villany,
In a short time he apprehended was
And brav'd His MAJESTY, even to his face
Yet when one wou'd have thought he shou'd have had
Reward for 's Villainy; and have been made
Example to all Ages our good KING
Gave him his life, (who long has strove to bring
Destruction on him,) and did him Restore
To liberty, thinking he ne'er wou'd more
Do anything unjust again when loe;
His stiring spirit, was not contented so
For he engages in th' conspiracy,
To Ruine th' Honour, Life and Liberty,
Of a deserving Noble, Honest Peer,
And him had brought unto destruction near
But Divine Providence for ever Blest:
Prevented this, as well as all the Rest
By th' coming in of some, that were concern'd
Which all your PLOT; into confusion turn'd,

At last our Famous HEROE Coronel BLOOD
Seeing his projects all will do no good,
And that Success was to him still deny'd
Fell sick with Grief, broke his Great Heart and dy'd.

The Epitaph.

HERE lies the Man who boldly hath run through
    More Villanies than ever ENGLAND knew
And nere to any friend he had was true
Here let him then by all unpittied lye
And let's Rejoyce his time was come to Dye.

Finis.

LONDON, Printed by J. S. in the year 1680.

N. B.—The Lutterell Collection of Broadsides in Large Room, British Museum. The above is No. 16 of the 1st of the three Volumes. It is encircled with or (perhaps better, surrounded by) a mourning edging ¾ inches deep, and on it has been added in contemporary MS. the date " 30th August, 1680," probably by the collector, indicating the date of its publication.

INTRODUCTION.

✐✐✐✐✐

To our trusty and well-beloved

Sir Rowland Edgerton
Bart.

◆

CHARLES R.

Trusty and well-beloved We greet you well, though we are unwilling in the last degree to presse upon our good subjects. Yet we must obey that Necessity which compells us in this publique Distraction when Our money and revenue is seized from us to lay hold on any thing wch with God's Blessing may be a means to preserve this

Kingdom. We must therefore desyre you forthwith to send us the somme of £2,000 for our necessary Support and the maintenance of Our Army, wch we are compelled to rayse for the defence of Our Person, the Protestant Religion, and the Laws of the Land. We have trusted this Bearer to receive it of you ; And We doe promise you in the word of a King to repay the same with Interest. And of this service We cannot doubt since if you should refuse to give Us this Testimony of yor Affection, you will give us too great cause to suspect yor Duty and Inclination both to Our Person and to the Publique Peace.

Given att Our Court att Oxford the 8th of February 1642.

Sir Rowland Edgerton Bart.

Colonel Blood.

THE above letter (beautifully written on parchment, and preserved in Warrington Museum) is a copy of a letter which the King issued from his Court at Oxford, to the gentry of this country, when he found that no further supply could be obtained from Parliament, and that Civil War was inevitable.

While the King, by this means, was making sure of their allegiance and support, and gathering together an army of excellent horsemen, the Parliament was collecting forces from the commoners, merchants and citizen classes. In every county there were two recruiting centres, the one endeavouring to carry out the order of Parliament, and the other the King's commission.

In Lancashire, the Earl of Derby as Lord Lieutenant, and Sir Thomas Tyldesley as Colonel, were the leaders of the Royalist party, and enlisted the services of Sir John Girlington, Alexander Rigby, Thomas Singleton, Butler, Whittingham, and other gentlemen, to whom commissions were given ; while Colonel Assheton was supported by Colonels Holcroft, Birch, Shuttleworth, Holland, Heywood, Starkie, etc., all county gentlemen, of good standing, and many of whom were members of Parliament.

Great sacrifices were made by Royalists to furnish the King with money to carry on the contest, many of them melting down their gold and silver plate into rough coin. The Queen herself journeyed to Holland to raise money on the Crown jewels.

At first, after raising the Royal Standard at Nottingham, the King, under the able commandership of the Princes Rupert and Maurice, and the gentry of Lancashire and Cheshire, had certainly the best of the contest. But as the nobility and gentry became poorer, and the King's supplies began to fail, the advantage turned to the other side, for the leaders of the Parliamentary party could obtain fresh supplies year after year by taxation.

The story which is about to be unfolded in this volume does not commence with the earlier battles and sieges of Edgehill, Brentford, Newbury, Marston Moor, Nazeby, Manchester, Liverpool, Lancaster, Preston, Wigan, Warrington, and Lathom, which took place between the two opposing parties up to 1648 ; but with the entrance of the Duke of Hamilton's forces into Lancashire, when Cromwell, with the young Lieutenant Blood, marched into Lancashire to oppose his advance, and when our hero (or villain some may call him) became acquainted with the family of Holcrofts, of Holcroft,

Culcheth, within a few miles of Winwick and Warrington, and from whence he married his bride. Only those events in Lancashire are recorded which took place during the period of the romance, and in which Blood or the family of the Holcrofts played some important part. To follow him in his adventurous career we must travel through a wide field of country as well as political history ; the period of history being, if not the most remarkable, at least the most changeable of our Empire.

Colonel Blood.

Part i.

Chapter i. Sketch of the early life and character of Lieutenant Blood —his introduction into the family of the Holcrofts— sketch of the life of Colonel Holcroft—his parliamentary career—his family and character of Maria Holcroft.

The Romance of

Chief Characters : COLONEL HOLCROFT.
THOMAS and MARIA.
LIEUTENANT BLOOD.

Colonel Blood.

CHAPTER I.

"The man had not only a daring, but a villainous, unmerciful look, a false countenance, but very well spoken, and dangerously insinuating."

SUCH was the character given by John Evelyn in his diary of the period in which the notorious Colonel Blood roamed the British Isles, and became the terror of his enemies, and the envy of his confederates. Ireland claims his birth, which was probably about 1630; and no one would doubt or dispute the fact of the Irish descent of one who by his desperate attempts at murder and robbery, his hairbreadth escapes from imprisonment

9

and justice, and his powers of impersonation, made his name and his villainy the talk of the Court of King Charles II. This I say, not because the Irish are more criminal than the English, or the rest of the civilized nations, but by reason of their extraordinary daring and courageous character in facing great odds, as seen in the late Boer War, and attempting deeds so dangerous and reckless that to others seem not only perilous but foolish.

His father during the reign of Charles I. had become a wealthy iron-master, and carried on his business in the shipping ports of the two countries. He was an ardent Protestant, and during the Civil Wars spent his fortune on the cause, and ended his days fighting with the Parliamentary forces. He had joined Fairfax, and helped him to raise that Army which was destined to change the Constitution from a Monarchy to a

Colonel Blood.

Commonwealth ; and by his influence obtained for his son Thomas a commission
under Fairfax as Lieutenant, though only
sixteen. So father and son fought side by
side in many of those engagements of the
South and West until a separation by death
came in 1645.

Thomas Blood had a great admiration for
Cromwell, and after his father's death joined
his forces, and soon became conspicuous as a
daring and courageous Lieutenant. He
marched North with Cromwell to meet the
Duke of Hamilton's forces, and was present
at the defeat of the Scotch Army at Preston,
Lancashire, when Cromwell, with Lambert,
routed the Scotch troops, and practically
ended the Civil War. It was at this time
that the romance of his life began, which is
a most interesting part of his career, and
which has not before been published.

Lieutenant Blood was tall, with a handsome dark face. We should say that he was "a dashing young officer," and "an ideal soldier." Like the rest of his Irish blood, he had the gift of wit and persuasive eloquence. During this Northern encounter he had met one Thomas Holcroft, a young man not much his senior, who had invited him to rest at Culcheth. At that time Colonel John Holcroft was the head of the Holcroft family, and Thomas his eldest son, and the family seat, Holcroft Hall.

The Holcrofts were of a most ancient and noble family. In the 13th century there lived one Gilbert de Culcheth, whose estates were extensive. He had four daughters, and to them he apportioned his estates. The eldest married Richard de Hindley, who took with the estate the family name of Culcheth. The second daughter was married to a brother of Richard, named Thomas, who took the name and the estate of Holcroft. The husband of the third became the owner of the estate, and head of the Pesfurlongs ; while the fourth brought her husband the name and estate of Risley.

At the time of our story Colonel John Holcroft was the owner of the Holcroft Estate, and his children were Thomas, Maria, Isabella, and Rachael. He was "a fine old English gentleman," and though loving a country life, and loath to leave his estate, he could not help joining the forces against the Royalists, together with the neighbouring gentlemen of the County. He had been M.P. for Liverpool in the Short Parliament, which sat from 13th April to May 5th, 1640.

In 1643 he raised, with Stanley, Egerton, and Holland, a troop, and fought the cause of Parliament for some years in and around Wigan and Warrington.[1]

He was present at the attack on Winwick Hall and Church. The Hall had been fortified by Sir John Fortesque, the Roman Catholic owner, who surrendered it to Colonels Holland and Holcroft. The taking of the Church was effected by the Parliamentary troops, commanded by Colonel Assheton, who had been joined by Holcroft. The Royalists had fortified the Church, and taken possession of it. The Parliamentary troops summoned them to surrender, and, shouting from the steeple, they agreed to surrender upon terms, which were refused by a volley from the troops, and one body fell headlong to the ground.[2]

He became Mayor of Liverpool in 1644. In 1645 M.P. for Wigan until 1648, when

---

[1] Appendix Note I. [2] Appendix Note II.

he was ejected under Pride's Purge. At this time he was parading and keeping the peace between Warrington and Culcheth and the surrounding districts of Lowton, Golborne, Ashton, as far as Wigan, and so fell in with Lieutenant Blood as Cromwell's forces were pursuing the Scotch troops.

Maria Holcroft, the eldest daughter of the Colonel, was tall and fair, with soft blue eyes. She had a pleasant face and was well proportioned. Pretty she was not. She was too masculine to be pretty. Determination was written upon her face. It was this characteristic which made her in after days so bravely fight the battle of life with such courage with the adventurous partner whose name and adventures became so notorious. She was now twenty. That was a great age, in those days, at which to arrive without being betrothed. It was customary for girls to marry at sixteen, and oftentimes before a girl had begun her teens her future husband had been chosen, not by herself, but her parents.

Colonel Holcroft had made up his mind that Maria should marry John Hulton, but Maria had also made up her mind, and she was determined to marry the dashing young Lieutenant. Colonel Holcroft had not liked all that he had seen of the young man, yet he had been forced by her determination to ask him to again visit Holcroft Hall. There was too much of the dare-devil talk about the Lieutenant for the Colonel. He had been brought up among the Culcheth folk all his life, and preferred to ride about his estate, drink his beer and sack, and think well of his neighbour. The thought of her attachment to this Lieutenant, of whom he knew nothing, was a trouble to him, and he

Colonel Blood.

longed for some unforseen event to occur to take the Lieutenant away from Holcroft for ever. Some sudden outbreak in the South which might take him there, or that he might be killed in the engagement with Hamilton's forces at Preston.

Part i.

The Romance of

Chief Characters: THE DUKE OF HAMILTON.
GENERAL CROMWELL.

CHAPTER II.

THE Duke of Hamilton marched from
Scotland, gathering in strength as he journeyed, so that by the time he had reached
Preston his troops numbered some twenty-
two thousands. Here he was to meet Sir
Marmaduke Langden's army. The account
of Cromwell meeting the two forces is so
well given in "A discourse of the Warr in
Lancashire," by an unknown author, and
written at the time, though it is generally
supposed to be a Major Edward Robinson,
of "Buckshawe," that I quote from it.

21

"Cromwell being come up with his forces into Yorkshire to Colonel Lambert, was at Knaresborough the 11th of August, and set from thence marching very sore every day. On the 14th day they came at night to Mr. Sherbourne's house, called Stonyhurst, about 'Hodder Watter,' where the General lodged that night, and his army encamped within the Park. Had a counsell of Warr that night, in which it was concluded to fight the Duke if he aboad. They followed in the reare of Sir Marmaduke Langden's Army, who came out of the North by Settletowne, and so into Blackburn Hundred, and through Ribchester, and downward to Preston. But some of them staying about the upper syd of ffulwood More and Ribbleton, lodged there that night.

"Cromwell made no stay, but in the morning marched on towards Preston after them, and when he was come as far as Ribbleton Mill there he found them. He set upon them fearsly, beating them all along the way to Preston (being three miles). Many were killed, some being trodden into the dirt in the Lanes with the horses' feet, the wayes were soe deep. Abundance were killed in the fieldes on the East syd of Preston, and so did drive them downe towards Ribble Bridge. The Duke, with his forces and carriages, being passed over before, having barocaded up the bridge, stood at resistance. It was reported that when word came to the Duke that General Cromwell was in the reare of Sir Marmaduke Langden's Army, fighting and killing them, his answer was, 'Let them alone; the English dogs are but killing one another.' So little care had he of them.

"At the Bridge they had a great dispute

for a long time, but at last Cromwell's Army did beat them off, and they fled over Darwen Bridge, and soe up that hill above Walton Towne. In the fielde upon the east of the way they made cabbins, and lodged there that night. Where the Duke quartered I heard not. So night coming, the armies guarded both ridges ; and General Cromwell returned to Preston, and there quartered, giving order to our Lancashire forces there to abide.

"And when morning was come with his armie he followed the Duke, who fled before him ; yet at some places made some stands as if they would fight it out, as upon Chorley More and Standish More ; but did not stand to it.

"The Scots were said to be greedie of plundering, though they were flying, for some of them were plundering the houses where Cromwell's men were killing some of their fellows without the doors. The greatest stand they made was between Newton and Winwick, in a straight passage in that lane that they made very strong and forcible, soe that Cromwell's men could not fight them. But by information of the people thereabouts, and by their direction they were soe guided into the fieldes that they came about so that they drove them up to that little Greene plot of ground short of Winwick Church, and there they made a great slaughter of them, and then pursued them to Warrington, there taking the most, if not all, of their Foot."[1]

The reader will, no doubt, be interested to read Cromwell's account of the battle, written from Warrington.

"The Honble. the Committee at Yorke.

[1] Appendix Note III.

"We have quite tyred our horses in 'pursuit' of the enemie. We have kill'd and dispers'd all their foot, and left them only some horse, with whom the Duke is fled into Dallaim's forest, having neither foot nor Dragoones. They have taken 500 of them.

"I mean the country forces, as they send me word this daye, they are so tyred, and in such confusion, that if my horse could but trott after them I could take them all; but we are soe weary we can scarce be able to doe more than walk after them. I beseech you, therefore, lett Sir Hen. Cholmdley, Sir Edward Roades, Coll. Hatcher, and Coll. Whyte, and all the cuntryes about you be sent too to ryse with you, and follow them, for they are the miserablest ptye that ever was. I durst engage myself with 500 fresh horse, and 500 nimble foot, to destroy them all: my horse are miserably beaten out, and

Colonel Blood.

I have 10,000 of them prisoners. Wee have kil'd wee know not what, but a very great number, having done execution upon them above 30 myles together, besides what we kil'd in the two great feights, the one at Preston, the other at Warrington.[1]

"The enemie was 24,000 horse, and foot, in the days of the feight, whereof 18,000 foot and 6,000 horse, and our number about 6,000 foot, and 3,000 horse·at the uttermost. This is a glorious daye. God helpe England to answer His mercies. I have noe more, but we beseech you, in all p'tes, to gather into bodies, and to pursew.

"I rest, your most humble servant,

"O. CROMWELL.

"Warrington, this 20th August, 1648.

"The greatest parte by far of the nobilitie of Scotland are with Duke Hambleton."

[1] Red Bank, Winwick.

The prisoners taken consisted of Lieutenant General Bayley, 5 colonels, 8 majors, 20 captains, 48 lieutenants, 78 ensigns, 3 quartermasters, 128 sergeants, and 2,256 private men. And if we are to take as true the statement made at the time, the fate of these prisoners was very hard. Thousands of them, it is said, were sent as slaves to Virginia and Barbadoes, and some even to the galleys in Venice.[1]

Cromwell returned from Warrington, intending to march again into Yorkshire. He therefore ordered all his forces with all haste to follow him to Stonyhurst, so that during one night all the troops had left the neighbourhood of Winwick and Warrington, Blood being hastily summoned from Holcroft Hall.

[1] Appendix Note IV.

Colonel Blood.

Part 1.

Chapter iii. Thomas Risley's interview with Colonel Holcroft — Lieutenant Blood's return to Holcroft Hall with the troopers.

The Romance of

Chief Characters: COLONEL HOLCROFT.
THOMAS RISLEY.
LIEUTENANT BLOOD.
MARIA HOLCROFT.

CHAPTER III.

The days had seemed long to Maria, as she anxiously waited for the return of the gay Lieutenant. Each day she listened for the sound of the troopers' horses, and when the news came that the Scottish troops had been routed, and followed to Wigan, and from thence to Winwick, she became excited, and bustled about and hurried the maids in the Hall with preparations for the advent of the troopers.

"What aileth thee, Maria?" said the Colonel as he noticed her activity among the maids.

31

"Dost thou not know that the troopers will be returning?" replied Maria.

"And what is that to thee?" said her father.

"But didst thou not bid them come this way if they had leisure?" answered Maria.

"Maybe I did," said her father; "for thou didst torment me with thy tongue, that I bid that fellow Blood return this way, if he had opportunity. But why hast thou set thy cap at him, as if thou hadst known him this many a year? He will do thee no good. He hath too handsome a face and too ready a tongue to please me. It would be well for thee to turn thy affection upon young Hulton."

"Did I not tell thee, father, that I would not marry John Hulton if he were as rich as Crœsus," said Maria.

She had from time to time been asked by

John Hulton, but neither his money nor his persistency had made her yield.

Her father was favourable to the match, and, indeed, had secretly arranged interview after interview for John Hulton to press his suit, but all to no avail.

"Marry John Hulton," she said, as she went off to inspect the rooms, and to see if all were ready for the troopers, "I would rather die the oldest maid in Culcheth than marry that soft lout with his gold."

The Colonel wished he had never seen the Lieutenant, and more than that, that he never asked him to return to Holcroft Hall.

He went out, much annoyed at his daughter's behaviour, saddled his mare, and rode towards Winwick to get further news of the rout of the Scotch forces.

He had not ridden far when he met his nephew, Thomas Risley, who greeted him with the words, "Good news, Uncle Holcroft. Thou wilt be glad to hear that the Roundheads have won the day. I wish I had been a soldier, rather than a student, to fight for truth and liberty. The Scots have been defeated, and the King will never reign again, for Parliament will banish him from the country."

"Thou art very well advised, Thomas. Thou art a Puritan, and thy speech savoureth of hatred to the King. Thou talkest like thy good father, who is ever complaining of the sin of the King," replied the Colonel.

"Nay, thou wrongest him, uncle. My father prayeth each day for the King," answered Thomas.

"Yea, I know he doth, but it is for his death," said the Colonel.

"Come, come, uncle, thou art not wont to speak like this. Art thou sorry that Cromwell has gained the day?" retorted Thomas.

34

"I am sorry the troopers ever came to Holcroft," answered the Colonel. "But hast thou seen ought of them in thy canter?" he asked.

"Indeed I have, for I have ridden fast to tell Maria that six troopers are coming to thy house. I met with them at Winwick. But not liking their company I bade them 'good day,' and hastened to tell of their coming," answered Thomas.

"Thou hast no need, for Maria is well prepared," said the Colonel. "But why didst thou not agree with thy company?" questioned he.

"Why, indeed! They prated of naught else but thy beer and sack and Maria. They are not good Roundheads or Puritans, for they spake nought of God being their helper and deliverer. The battle, they said, was won by their own strength, and they boasted that they had sent some hundreds to hell, when it was all in the hands of God. They enquired of me concerning thee and Maria, and one said he would carry off Maria, and marry her. While another said he would fill his belly with thy sack. And another impudent fellow asked me what fortune thou wouldst give to Maria when she were wed," replied Thomas.

"Thou hast wisely left thy company, Thomas," said the Colonel.

He turned his horse's head, and started back for Culcheth. He would have taken Thomas home with him, for he and Maria were good friends, and he had often declared that when he became a goodly Rector he would wed Maria. But Thomas was anxious to make known the news to his father, who, though professing loyalty to the King, had strong views with regard to religion, and regretted the action of Archbishop Laud in trying to force the Church's doctrine upon the Scottish nation. He now leaned towards Presbyterianism, and was constantly instilling into the minds of his sons the dangers of the Roman Catholic influence in the country. This warning had its effect in after years, as we shall see in the course of the story.

As soon as the Colonel arrived at Holcroft Hall he informed Maria of the news, and added : " I pray thee, daughter, keep thy head clear and thy heart safe, for these troopers are not good and faithful men. I met thy cousin, Thomas Risley, coming to warn thee of their impudence. They have sworn to carry thee away, and marry thee."

" I have not lived a maid these twenty years to be carried off against my will," replied Maria.

" But thou art not too old or too poor to

make these fools quarrel and fight for thy dowry," answered her father. "I warrant thee thou wilt not have an easy time with their flattering tongues."

"Thou art prating aforetime," said Maria, who was annoyed at her father's warning. "Where did Thomas meet the troopers?" she asked.

"They are on their way from Winwick, where Cromwell is resting his troops," replied her father.

With this answer Maria ran off to the servants' hall, and busied herself preparing food for the coming guests, while her father went to the stables to make accommodation for the six extra horses.

Within an hour of the Colonel's return the troopers had arrived, and with them his son Thomas, who had joined them on the way.

"Good day, Master Holcroft, we have

returned to thy hospitality," said one of the troopers as he dismounted.

"We have not fed with ease these ten days," said another.

"Nor drunk to quench a sick man's thirst," said a third.

"I remember that thou had'st some rare sack, Master Holcroft," said a fourth.

"We must drink to the cause of liberty," continued the fifth.

Thomas Holcroft took the lead into the Hall, and the Colonel bid the guests welcome to rest, and called Maria to give the troopers their fill of ale and sack.

Maria's eyes caught the young Lieutenant's as he came in, and as she gave him a welcome smile, she said, " Thou art welcome, Master Blood. We are glad to greet thee after thy hard riding. I am glad that thy bones were not broken, or that thy body was not left on the battlefield. Thou must tell us of the fighting."

"Right gladly will he tell thee, girl," said her brother, "for he has talked oft of thee along the way.

"Ah! now I see the blush! Away with thee, sister, and bid the maids bring some refreshment."

The Colonel did not favour the speech of his son. His manners since his connection with the troopers had not pleased his father, and what with Maria's amiability to the Lieutenant, and his son's friendliness towards him, his heart was filled with fear.

The young Lieutenant said very little until they had supped, and when Maria came and sat with the rest of the company, she was so fascinated and charmed with the accounts of his adventures — his narrow escapes from death and his reckless courage

Colonel Blood.

—that Maria that night—on retiring to rest, dreamt that the Lieutenant was killed on the battlefield, and that his dead body was being trampled upon by galloping horses.

The sound of the horses in the stable yard awakened her, and right glad she felt when the morning revealed it was but a dream.

For three days the company remained at the Hall, and each day Maria's love grew stronger as nightly she listened to his voice, which sang and spoke of love in every breath. When the time came to say good-bye, Maria had thrown her father's warning aside, and completely lost her head, and given her heart away to the young Lieutenant.

Part i.

Chapter iv. The story of Pride's Purge
— the trial and Execution
of Charles I.

The Romance of

Chief Characters: CHARLES I.
COLONEL PRIDE.
COLONEL HOLCROFT.
CROMWELL, BRADSHAW AND
COKE.

CHAPTER IV.

THE battle of Winwick finally settled any further chance of King Charles being either restored to the throne or to freedom. It was the "last straw" which sealed his fate. From that day Cromwell's adherents said "so long as Charles Stuart lives, there will be no peace in the land." They were determined that Charles should be brought openly to trial, as a traitor to his country.

Cromwell knew that the nation in secret had been turning towards the Captive King, and that many members of the House of

Commons would never consent to his death. He therefore sent Colonel Ewer, who had fought in Ireland and had been at the siege of Drogheda with him, to take the King from the charge of Colonel Hammond at Carisbrook Castle (of whom Cromwell had suspicions that he was aiding the King to escape), and to bring him to Hurst Castle to be under closer supervision.

It is hard to lay the blood of King Charles on Cromwell's memory, yet we cannot doubt but that one with so much power could have saved his head if he had wished. And when he resorted to such drastic measures of what is known as "Pride's Purge" to pass the Act stating that it was treason to raise an army or to fight against Parliament, he was guilty of committing a similar act to that which had brought such censure upon the King.

46

Colonel Blood.

The Parliament had declared by a majority of forty-six in favour of the Newport Treaty which was the last negotiation between the King and Parliament : but on the following day Colonel Pride was ordered to station himself at the door of the House of Commons ; and as each member, who had voted for the Newport Treaty or who was known to have been friendly to the King, approached, he was either carried off to prison by the troopers or forbidden to enter the House. Over a hundred were excluded, among whom was Colonel Holcroft, who (though a staunch Parliamentarian) was not a party to that deed which is one of the saddest and darkest pages of English history. The Colonel had never wished to enter the Army, but he was forced by the political situation of the time to take one side or the other, because of his position in the County.

As he could not join with the Earl of Derby and Sir Thomas Tyldesley in supporting the King because he did not agree with the manner in which he ruled his country, he must necessarily join the Roundheads. And it is to his credit as a fine old English gentleman that he never soiled his hand by signing the death warrant of the King.

The fifty members of Parliament who thus passed the act accusing the King of treason, were afterwards spoken of as " The Rump," and they were at the mercy of the New Army, and passed whatever was put forward by them. On the 7th of December, 1648, the King was brought by Colonel Harrison from Hurst Castle to Whitehall, to await his trial, the verdict of which had already been settled by Cromwell and the New Army. On New Year's Day, 1649, it was declared by Parliament, that to levy war against it was

48

High Treason, and a High Court of Justice was appointed to decide whether Charles had been guilty of that treason or not. The House of Lords, consisting chiefly of officers of the Army, had the courage to refuse to take part in the proceedings, but the Commons determined to act upon their own authority. On the 20th of January, the High Court, self-created and self-styled, assembled in the Painted Chamber at Westminster Hall. Bradshaw sat as President, and Coke acted as the solicitor for the nation. With all the solemn apparatus of a Court of Justice, the trial, which was a mockery and a farce, as the verdict had already been determined before the trial commenced, dragged on for seven days. Never did the King appear to more advantage than at this mockery of a trial. Arousing all his kingly dignity, of which he possessed no small share, he said he refused to be tried by a tribunal created in the defiance of the laws. By the letter of the law the King was right ; but Bradshaw replied that " no court would allow its own jurisdiction to be questioned." In vain did Charles plead for a conference with a joint committee of Lords and Commons, but they would not agree, and as he still refused to plead, the death sentence was passed on the seventh day. During the trial, he had been exposed to many insults and upbraidings, which he bore with beautiful calmness and dignity. As the trial was proceeding, the real feelings of the people became more and more apparent. From time to time the crowd burst forth into " God save the King ! " " Good King Charles ! " " Down with the Army ! " and it was evident that the hearts of the English people were returning to their King in the days of his downfall and misery.

Colonel Blood.

Only sixty-seven members out of one hundred and thirty-four summoned to the Court, were present when the King's condemnation was pronounced. Fifty-nine of them, among whom was General Cromwell and Colonel Jones, signed the death Warrant.

On the 30th, in front of his own Palace of Whitehall, a scaffold had been erected. Soldiers, horse and foot, surrounded the black platform, on which stood two masked headsmen beside the block. The crowds stood in silence, not daring to utter a word of loyalty for fear of the soldiers. As the King came forth attended by Bishop Juxon, his behaviour was firm and yet gentle. Standing before the people, he said, "Sirs, it is for the liberties of the people that I am come here; if I would have assented to an arbitrary sway, to have all things changed according to the power of the sword, I needed not to have come hither, and therefore I tell you, and I pray God it be not laid to your charge, that I am a martyr to the people." He also declared that the guilt of the civil war did not rest with him, for the Parliament had been first to take up arms; but confessing at the same time that he was now suffering a just punishment for the death of Strafford. He seemed glad to have done with all his earthly troubles, and remarked a few minutes before receiving the stroke of the executioner's axe, "I go from a corruptible to an incorruptible crown, where no disturbance can be." One blow from the axe, and all was over. When the royal head, grey with the cares of many troubled years, fell on the scaffold, a deep groan of compassion arose from the thousands of spectators who thronged round the scaffold. And when the executioner raised the dripping

Colonel Blood.

head and cried, "This is the head of a traitor," the women hid their faces, while the men cried, "Shame!" "Shame!" "God save the King!" That day, in many a sturdy English heart, among which were those of Colonels Holcroft and Birch, was felt the true manly sorrow for the nation's guilt in thus bringing the royal head to the dust. Since the conquest, five kings have fallen by assassination; three have died of injuries received in battle; once only has a king of England perished on the scaffold, and this chapter tells the dark and bloody tale.

Part i.

The Romance of

Chief Characters: GENERAL CROMWELL.
GOVERNOR ASTON.
COLONEL JONES.
LIEUTENANT BLOOD.

CHAPTER V.

LIEUTENANT BLOOD was ordered out with
Cromwell's forces to Ireland. It was the
year 1649. Ireland was at this time un-
decided in its attitude towards the Parliament,
and great hopes were entertained by the
Royalists that that country might be the
rallying ground of their forces. The death
of Charles I. had the effect of re-establishing
the Royalists, and the Duke of Ormond
returning under the title of Lord Lieutenant
had healed the contentions of the many
factions which were then rife in that quarrel-
some country.

57

Lord Inchiquin, who had just defeated the Royalists' troops at Clontarf, now joined the Duke, and the famous O'Neil's Irish force gave their voice and swords for the Royalists. Only Dublin, Londonderry, and Belfast of the large towns remained faithful to Parliament. The Duke, with collected forces, marched to Dublin to complete the triumph of his victories, but contrary to expectation, he was defeated by Michael Jones, and his scattered forces followed to Rathmines, where, on August 2nd, his army was completely destroyed. On July 12th Cromwell set out for Bristol with unwonted state, in a coach drawn by six grey Flanders mares, and protected by a life guard, every member of which was "either an officer or a squire."

Above him floated a milk-white standard, symbolising, as it would seem, "to bring back white-robed Peace from amidst the horrors of war." He arrived in Bristol two days after, but was not able to start for a considerable length of time until a sufficient supply was promised by Parliament. The money having arrived, he was able to encourage the troops, who had grown troublesome and rebellious, and he set sail on August 13th, for Dublin.

The first news that greeted Cromwell on his arrival was that the Duke of Ormond had reinforced the garrison of Drogheda, and that Michael Jones had been repulsed in an attempt to surprise the town. He, therefore, set out for Drogheda, and on the 3rd of September, his whole army numbering ten thousand, laid siege to the town. On the 10th he summoned Aston, the Governor, to surrender, and refusing, Cromwell started a steady cannonade, and by evening he had destroyed the steeple of the church, and made a breach in the walls. The following day he gave orders to storm the city, and three regiments—those of Ewer, Hewson, and Castle—rushed up the perilous slope, and endeavoured to surmount the fragments of the broken wall. Twice they were hurled back with loss. Then Cromwell himself, having chosen Colonel Jones, Lieutenant Blood, and a few other officers, leapt forward to head the baffled column to one last attempt. Encouraged by their commander, they bravely poured over the broken rampart and took the city.

The mass of the defeated garrison fled hurriedly down the sloping streets to gain the bridge, and then the terrible and lasting blot upon a character so great and courageous was committed—the massacre of four thousand of the garrison. "The deed was all his own. Till he spoke the words of fate the soldiers were breaking down the defences, and some were offering quarter to its defenders. Cromwell's order of 'no quarter' put an end to these proffers of mercy, and, with few exceptions, the Royalists were butchered as they stood. The head of Aston (the Governor of the town) was beaten in with his own wooden leg, which the soldiers had torn away in the belief that he had concealed treasure in it. (After his death, however, two hundred gold pieces were found in his girdle). Still Cromwell's wrath was not satiated. In the heat of passion there stood out in his mind, through the blood red haze of war, thoughts of vengeance to be taken for the Ulster massacre, confusedly mingled with visions of peace more easily secured by instant severity. The stern command to put all to the sword who were in arms leapt lightly from his lips.

"Then ensued a scene the like of which had seldom been witnessed in an English war. Amidst shrieks and groans, and shouts of triumph, pike and sword plied their fiendish work down the sloping street. The flying wretches were in no case to block the narrow passage of the bridge, and the slaughter continued as pursuers and pursued breasted the steep hill on the northern side of the Boyne. A thousand were slain in and around St. Peter's Church, at the top of the hill. When Cromwell came up he found that about eighty had taken refuge in the steeple. These he summoned to surrender to mercy, and, hopeless as their position was, they refused the offer. After a fruitless attempt to blow up the tower with gunpowder. Cromwell gave orders to drag the seats in the church beneath it, and to set them on fire, As the flames gained the structure above, the unhappy victims attempted to escape to the roof. Some fifty were killed, while the remaining thirty perished in the flames of the burning steeple, some of them cursing the souls of the enemy as they were burning. What was worse, even the few who, by the connivance of the soldiers, had escaped death on the Mill Mount, were sought out, and killed in cold blood, while the rest of the civilians were made prisoners, and sent to Barbadoes." This terrible slaughter caused panic in the Royalist forces, but gave the troopers a thirst for blood. The thirst could not be quenched. Garrisons were put to the sword, and whole towns left unpeopled as the army marched its bloody way.

At Wexford, on October 12th, the same measures were meted out to the garrison as at Drogheda. "The soldiers and townsmen who resisted, after the walls were scaled, were put to the sword, and here, too, the priests and friars were butchered without mercy. Some of the men, hoping to move the infuriated soldiery to mercy, approached them with crucifixes in their hands, and were at once put to death as idolaters. Others in their rush to the water's edge, found themselves in the midst of a struggling multitude of men and women. All who could threw themselves into the boats, but boats, pressed down by an agonised crowd, could not long float, and it was reckoned that about 300 were drowned. Every friar in the town was knocked on the head, and a few civilians perished, either being mistaken for soldiers, or through the mere frenzy of the conquerors." By the end of the year the whole of the South had practically been conquered. The next year saw Kilkenny taken, the county of Tipperary devastated, and the capture of

Colonel Blood.

Clonmell.   This was the last feat of arms for Cromwell in Ireland.   On May 26th, leaving Ireton as Lord Deputy, he sailed for Bristol, and on June 1st he was received with a hearty welcome on Hounslow Heath, and a grant of land and a house, opposite Whitehall, given him for his residence.   Colonel Jones and Blood, with the title "Colonel," crossed over to England with him.

Part i.

Chapter vi. Colonel Blood's visit to
Holcroft and his account
of the siege of Drogheda
—his meeting with Maria
and proposal.

The Romance of

Chief Characters: Colonel and Thomas Holcroft
Colonel Blood and Maria.

CHAPTER VI.

It was not long ere Colonel Blood made
his way once more to Culcheth. News
travelled very slowly in those days, and love
letters were not sent every day, as now.
The swiftest carrier was the noble steed, and
the safest postman the lover himself. Blood
rode with all haste to Holcroft. Thomas
was the first to see him, and thought he was
a messenger with dispatches from Parliament.

"Who can the messenger be!" he said
to himself, as he stood straining his eyes
towards Culcheth, trying to discover from
the dress or the steed the desperate rider.

"It favours young Blood," he said, "but that cannot be. He would not be allowed to leave so early. It is only a few days ago that I heard Cromwell had returned."

Nearer and nearer came the rider, and each moment brought the features clearer.

"'Pon my soul, it is Blood," he said. "By my life, I know not how he has come so quickly."

"Welcome, thrice welcome ; thou hast lost no time in coming ! I warrant it's a woman that has brought thee so swiftly," said Thomas.

"Thou art right, Master Holcroft ; and where is Maria ?" answered Blood.

"She is in safe keeping," replied Thomas, "and thou canst feast thine eyes upon her as long as thou wilt, if thou wilt get thee from that sweltering mare."

"Here, take this mare," said Thomas,

turning to a stable boy, "and see that she is well groomed and covered."

"Come now, tell me, how goes the war, and what has brought thee back so soon?" he said as they entered the Hall. "I only heard this day week that Cromwell was returned."

"Cromwell has returned and I with him," replied Blood, "and here I am to claim the lady who bid me hasten back."

"And thou canst have her, sir," said Thomas. "I will give her thee in yon church whene'er thou choosest."

"Bridget, go tell Maria that Master Blood is here."

"Colonel," interrupted Blood.

"What! Colonel! didst thou say? I beg thee a thousand pardons," said Thomas.

But Bridget had bounded off to tell her young mistress of her lover's return.

They were then joined by Colonel Holcroft, who had overheard the last part of their conversation.

"Thou hast well earnt thy title, I warrant," said the Colonel. "Thy sword has not been idle, or thy brains, if forsooth, the news is true."

"The news is only too true. Cromwell hath a hard heart, and an iron will," said Blood. "He hath no mercy for his victims. He would kill his mother, I trow, if she were a Papist; and while he kills he prays. I fear 'twill be long ere his name is forgotten in yon Isle. The blood flowed in the streets of Drogheda like water, and my arms ached for days. I warrant I killed two score or more."

"Right glad I am he has left me here to keep the peace in Culcheth," replied the Colonel.

Colonel Blood.

"Thou hast a quiet and peaceful heart," said Blood. "Men like Cromwell and thy humble guest thirst for conquest. There is no quarter where there is blood to spill. It is better to kill thine enemy, or perchance he will kill thee."

"Thou truly hast a thirst for conquest, but I am best pleased when there is no blood to spill," said the Colonel. "But here comes Maria. We will leave thee; for I would not spoil thy greeting after so long absence."

Neither will we venture to describe their greeting.

> Let it suffice that each had charms,
> He clasped a goddess in his arms;
> And though she felt his usage rough,
> Yet in a man 'twas well enough.
> *Goldsmith.*

Blood, though a reckless trooper, was an honourable lover. He wooed and won Maria Holcroft in all good faith; and none could have foretold anything but a happy wedded life. Yet beneath that handsome dark face was a cold-blooded heart, and one that never forgave an injury.

Soon the story of love was told.

So, with the promise of Thomas to give her away as soon as he wished, he took courage, and asked her to name the day. With girl-like coquettishness she hesitated, and bade him ask again.

They were joined by Thomas, who, in his lively manner and chaffing voice, said, "Well, ye doves, have ye not done cooing yet? When have ye settled for the wedding?"

"We haven't settled yet," said Maria, and with this reply she fled from the room.

"Thou hast not succeeded," said Thomas. "Leave her to herself, and she will tell thee, I wager. When hast thou to return?" he asked.

74

Colonel Blood.

"This day month," answered Blood.

"And hast thou a cage to put thy bird in ?" asked Thomas.

"I have not," replied Blood, "for I cannot vouch how long I shall tarry in Ireland. I have the command of a regiment under Ireton, and if these rebels are either killed or sent to Barbadoes, I may return in six months."

"And if thou art alive," interrupted Thomas, "but I will see Maria and the Colonel, and thou shalt have thine answer and the Colonel's consent."

Part 1.

Chapter vii. The meeting of the rival lovers and the invitation to the wedding.

The Romance of

Chief Characters: COLONEL BLOOD.
                    THOMAS HOLCROFT.
                    THOMAS RISLEY.

CHAPTER VII.

On the morrow, Thomas Holcroft and Colonel Blood rode out towards Winwick, and close by Southworth Hall they met Thomas Risley, who has already been made known to the reader.

"Hey day! Thomas," said Holcroft. "Come, speak to Colonel Blood."

"We have met before, Cousin," said Risley, and turning to Blood, said, "I wish thee well, Colonel."

"Did we not meet on this way before?" asked the Colonel.

"I warrant we did, and thou didst enquire

79

of my uncle, Colonel Holcroft, and Maria," answered Risley.

"Thou sayest rightly; it was just after the defeat of Hamilton," replied Blood.

"Come, congratulate the Colonel," said Thomas Holcroft, "he is going to wed Maria."

"This is strange news, forsooth," said Risley; "but I wish them well. Maria hath a stout heart and a determined will, and will make thee as fine a mate as thou couldst find in Lancashire," he said to Blood.

"He has stolen a march on thee, Thomas," said Holcroft.

"I wager he hath," answered Risley; but he hath a trooper's coat, and I a plain broadcloth."

"Thou sayest naught of good looks," said Blood.

"There thou hast advantage again; for while I have the fair and blue eyes of a

Saxon, thou hast the dark hair and brown eyes of a Norman," replied Risley; "thou wast born to conquer, and I to serve."

"Bravely said," answered Blood, "but thou wilt serve thy country with thy words, as nobly as I serve it with my sword, I warrant."

"God grant that it may be so," said Risley.

"Yet I fear man is ever wont to fight more with his sword than with his tongue."

"The tongue is a woman's weapon," said Holcroft, "and I warrant Maria will make him feel it ere long."

"Happy is the man who feels Maria's tongue. I would bear a thousand lashes from it, could I but have her love," said Risley.

"Come, spare thy feelings, cousin, it cannot be. Maria hath this very morn told me she will wed the Colonel on the 21st," said Holcroft. "But thou wilt come to church, and see thy cousin wed."

"No, Thomas, I could not see her wed another man. I wish them well; but I can but envy the man who carries off the prize," answered Risley.

"Thou art a simpleton, cousin! But, tell thy father and mother we bid them to the wedding," said Holcroft, as they cantered off.

Thomas Risley went home broken-hearted. Colonel Blood had stolen Maria's heart from him, and she was now lost to his life. He had just begun his studies at Pembroke College, Oxford, but here was a blow which for the time being seemed to cast all ambition and hope aside.

Maria would not have made a curate's wife, though on one occasion in after years she assumed that character, and played that part. Her love was too romantic for the life of quiet self-denial, of silent poverty, which are the virtues of the curate's wife, whose heart and life are devoted to her husband's cause.

"What aileth thee, Thomas?" said his father, as he sat looking disconsolate and full of trouble.

"What aileth me?" he answered, in troubled surprise. "Did I not tell thee that one of those troopers whom I met going to Uncle John's said he would carry off Maria. Maria is to be wed on the 21st to that very man. I met cousin Thomas and this Colonel Blood this morn, and he bid me to the wedding, and said, 'Tell thy father and mother that Maria and I bid them to the church.'"

"This is indeed ill news," said his mother. "I would rather she had wed some one with a good name."

"I wish she had ne'er seen that trooper," said Thomas.

"Keep thy heart with all diligence, we read in that precious Word," said his father.

"For out of it are the issues of life and death," added Thomas. For at that moment, Thomas thought death was preferable to life. He had quietly loved his cousin Maria, and had hoped that when he had been ordained he would wed her. But now death would happily be endured, for all hope had gone, and life would be different without those loving thoughts of Maria.

In after years, as he heard from time to time of the life she was leading with him who was once the handsome young Lieutenant, but now the greatest desperado of the reign, he thought what a different life she might have led had not fate decreed otherwise.

Colonel Blood.

Part 1.

Chapter viii. The wedding of Colonel Blood and Maria at Newchurch, and the prophecy of the Rev. William Leigh.

The Romance of

Chief Characters: COLONEL BLOOD AND MARIA.
THOMAS HOLCROFT AND ELEANOR
BIRCH.
THE REV. WILLIAM LEIGH.

CHAPTER VIII.

On the 21st of June, 1650, the church at Culcheth (called Newchurch) was the scene of one of the most lamentable, and yet, perhaps, the happiest days of Maria's life ; lamentable because of the after results ; and the happiest because she had married the man of her choice.[1] Yet there was a sadness in the loneliness of the wedding. What might have been a scene of brilliancy and gaiety, and a gathering together of the

[1] Thomas Bloud gens et Maria Holcroft matrimonio copulati vicessimo primo die Junni anno Domi, 1650.—Newchurch Registers.

county families of south-west Lancashire, was turned into a solemn and dismal scene of six standing before the altar. Colonel Holcroft absolutely refused to witness it. William Leigh,[1] the curate of Newchurch, was the officiating minister, and was included in the small gathering at the wedding feast at Holcroft Hall. The only stranger or representative of the county families was Eleanor Birch, of Birch, a lifelong friend of Maria's, who, with Thomas Holcroft and his two sisters, were the only witnesses of that eventful marriage.

The Rev. William Leigh and Thomas Holcroft were the merriest, if not the happiest, of the gathering at the banquet table, and towards evening, as the day seemed to drag, the three young men, Colonel Blood, Thomas Holcroft, and the Rev. William

[1]Appendix Note V.

Leigh sat conversing of anything and everything, except the wedding.

"I wager, Master Holcroft, that there will be another wedding in this house ere another year has passed," said the Rev. William Leigh.

"Then it will be thyself," replied Thomas Holcroft, "for I saw Eleanor Birch making eyes at thee all this even."

"Then it is because thou art so smitten with her that thou couldst not let thine eyes go from following her," answered William Leigh. "I wager that if God and Parliament keep me at Newchurch I will wed thee to Eleanor Birch."

"Thou shalt have the finest bottle of port thou hast ever tasted if thou art right," replied Holcroft.

"Then I will have thy wine, forsooth," answered William Leigh.

Eleanor Birch was the daughter of Thomas Birch, of Birch, and had for many years been intimate with the Holcrofts. She was Maria's one friend, and had frequently visited her at Holcroft Hall, her father's home. There had sprung up between Thomas Holcroft and Eleanor a friendship, in which no mention of love had ever occurred. But now he had settled at Holcroft Hall, and had an ample allowance from his father, he could, therefore, enter seriously in the cause of matrimony, and that day his mind and his heart were set upon Eleanor Birch.

Maria's marriage was, by everyone except herself, considered to be unfortunate and unwise. Though Thomas Holcroft, her brother, had given his sister that day to the care and keeping of Colonel Blood, yet the fact of knowing that on all sides the union was unacceptable, made him regret somewhat his light-heartedness and his ready willingness in bringing about this speedy and romantic marriage.

The time was not long ere it expired for the return of the Colonel to Ireland. He left Culcheth, not realising that two years would pass before he again saw Maria or Holcroft. In the peaceful and quiet home she spent the next two years, but meanwhile she became the mother of a son.[1] It was not until the wedding of Thomas Holcroft and Eleanor Birch that Colonel Blood set his eyes upon his first-born, and visited Holcroft again.

---

[1] Thomas filius Thome Blood ari. baptizatus 30mo Martii anno Domi, 1651.—Newchurch Parish Registers.

Part i.

Chapter ix. Prince Charlie gathers together an Army and marches through Lancashire and Cheshire on to Worcester without opposition.

The Romance of

Chief Characters: PRINCE CHARLES.
SIR THOMAS TYLDESLEY.
MAJOR GENERAL LAMBERT.
THE YOUNG GENTLEMEN OF
PRESTON.

CHAPTER IX.

Just two days after the wedding, Charles II. landed in Scotland. A joyous welcome was given him at Edinburgh, and for some months he remained there until the city was taken by Cromwell. He, however, escaped, and rallied the scattered forces which had been defeated at Dunbar on September 3rd, 1650, and he was crowned at Scone on New Year's Day, 1651. He then advanced south as Cromwell moved northward, and gathering forces as he came, he crossed the border with at least 16,000. A dispatch was sent to the

95

Earl of Derby, who sailed from the Isle of Man while Charles marched with Sir Thomas Tyldesley, without opposition, right into Lancashire, through Preston and Wigan, staying on the 15th of August at Bryn, the seat of Sir William Gerard, and on through Warrington into Cheshire, where on the 17th, near Northwich, he had an interview with the Earl. It was one of the strangest mysteries how the young King was allowed to march so quietly through Lancashire, but a writer has quaintly stated that "His army marched through the county, carrying very faire and peaceably, without plundering or any other violence, all the county through, not offering to force or compell any to comply or joyn with them unless they voluntarily offered themselves, only provision for their army was required in a faire and mild way. This faire carrying tooke much with the county, and won their hearts so farr that many said, and were well persuaded they would prevaile, their candour and carriage was soe amiable. They made noe stay or abode in any place over a night or two. The young King rode through Preston, mounted on horse backe, and they said he rode through every streete to be seen of the people. Yet it was observed that he received small entertainment there, only one woman who seemed to show more respect to him than all the towne besides, which, it was said, was some greefe to him. Hee was well nigh through Lancashire when the Earle of Darbie landed."

The young King had been followed by Major-General Lambert from Scotland, who had arrived at Warrington before the King's forces, but he did not force a battle. He marched before them as far as Knutsford

Heath, the Scots charging his reare from time to time, but were beaten off with very little loss. He then turned aside, and let them pass, following after them to Worcester. Meanwhile the Earl of Derby and Sir Thomas Tyldesley were raising a force for the King in Lancashire, making Preston their headquarters. Their actions were carefully watched by a regiment of horse, and two or three of foot, commanded by Colonel Holcroft and others from the neighbourhood, till Colonel Lilburne came near to Preston with his horse, where he quartered at Brindle, grazing his horses between the church and Preston town. An event interesting to the locality of Preston occurred during the night. Twenty or more young gentlemen, hearing that the horses were grazing, and that the men were asleep, without order made a foolish attempt to capture some of the horses.

Colonel Blood.

They got into the meadows where the horses were feeding without being heard, and were tying the horses together, when an alarm was given. A fight followed, and only one of the young men escaped, named Newsham, who fled, and hid in the woods, or, as the historian says, "in a thick oller tree" until night, and then escaped. "Butler, the young heir of Ratcliffe, and Hesketh, a second son of Mr. Hesketh, of Maynes, were killed, and a few others, while the rest were made prisoners."

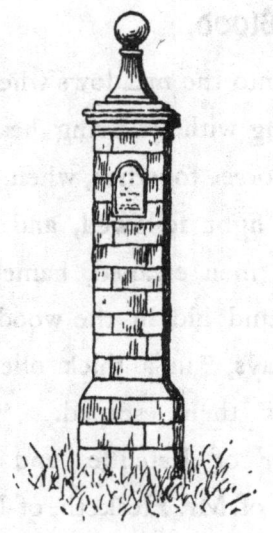

An high Act of Gratitude, which conveys the Memory of
SIR THOMAS TYLDESLEY,
To posterity,
Who served KING CHARLES THE FIRST as Lieutenant-Colonel
At Edge-Hill Battle,
After raising Regiments of Horse, Foot, and Dragoons,
And for
The desperate storming of Burton-upon-Trent, over a bridge of 36 arches
RECEIVED THE HONOUR OF KNIGHTHOOD.
He afterwards served in all the wars in great command,
Was Governor of Lichfield,
And followed the fortune of the Crown through the Three Kingdoms,
And never compounded with the Rebels, though strongly invested
And on the 25th August, A.D. 1651, was here slain,
Commanding as Major General under the EARL OF DERBY,
To whom the grateful Erector, ALEXANDER RIGBY, Esq.,
was Cornet;
And when he was High Sheriff of this County (A.D. 1679),
Placed this high obligation on the whole
FAMILY OF THE TYLDESLEYS, to follow the noble example of
Their Loyal Ancestor.

Part i.

Chapter i. An account of the great battle at Wigan Lane, where the Earl of Derby's forces were cut up by Colonels Lilburne and Holcroft, Captains Jollie and Smith—the death of Sir Thomas Tyldesley and the slaughter of the escaped Scots from Worcester.

The Romance of

Chief Characters:

Royalists—	Parliamentarians—
THE EARL OF DERBY.	COLONEL LILBURNE.
SIR THOMAS TYLDESLEY.	COLONEL HOLCROFT.
SIR WILLIAM WITHERINGTON.	CAPTAIN JOLLIE.
SIR WILLIAM THROCMORTON.	CAPTAIN SMITH.
SIR T. FEATHERSTON HAUGH.	
COLONEL BOYNTON.	

CHAPTER X.

COLONEL LILBURNE removed his quarters a
little further from Preston, only to find on
the following morning that the Earl and his
troops had secretly marched from Preston.
He quickly followed them to within a mile
and a half of Wigan, determined to attack.
But before he had laid his plans the Earl and
his army came out "from Wiggon towne's
end, all along that broad sandie loane up to
that loane end which goeth towards Mr.
Bradshaw's House at Hay," the horsemen
lining the hedges as he advanced with his

infantry. They were saluted with a galling fire of musketry from the Parliamentarians, but not heeding the dreadful and deadly fire, they advanced again, and were met with another volley. They then halted, and divided into companies, he, the Earl, commanding the van, and Sir Thomas Tyldesley the rear. A charge was then sounded, and with a fierce determination and a courage which was inspired by their faithful commanders, they advanced, and cut through the main body, driving Lilburne's forces almost "to that loane end that goes to Hay." Again they charged, and again cut through the enemy, but not without heavy loss. Twice the Earl had his horse shot from under him and Colonel Boynton and Major-General Sir William Witherington were wounded. A third time they charged, but they were met with overwhelming and unequal numbers, for Lilburne had been reinforced, and the horse coming up drove the Earl's army before them, the Earl himself receiving a blow on the face. He fled from the battlefield, and took refuge in a house in the market place until his wound was dressed, and then fled. Sir Thomas Tyldesley, now left in command, fought bravely, and with the fierceness of a gallant noble leader in a lost cause. He determined to sell his life dearly, and not to leave the field till his dead body was carried to its last resting place. Colonel Holcroft and Captains Jollie and Smith, with their companies, cut up the defeated forces as they pursued them, and took over 400 prisoners.[1] Besides Sir Thomas Tyldesley, both Colonel Boynton and Major-General Sir William Witherington were slain.

[1] Appendix Note VI.

There was no more zealous commander of the King's forces in Lancashire than Sir Thomas Tyldesley. He began life as a soldier, and from the commencement of the Civil War he entered into the conflict with a gallantry and enthusiasm which was equalled by none, not even the noble Earl of Derby. Indeed, it is said it was he who fired the first shot, and drew the first blood in the county when he was being entertained at the house of a Mr. Greene, in Manchester. Hearing a man proclaiming in favour of the Parliament, a shot came forth from the window of Mr. Greene's house, and killed the man on the spot. A second shot was fired at Mr. Birch, afterwards Colonel Birch, but he escaped by hiding himself under a cart. Sir Thomas then fled from Manchester to Wigan, and began to train the recruits in preparation for the coming conflict, in which he played a conspicuous part until his death. He was knighted for his services at the storming of the bridge at Burton. In 1644 he was taken prisoner at the battle of Montgomery, and afterwards escaped, when the King appointed him Governor of Lichfield, which town he surrendered on articles on 16th July, 1646. He was afterwards appointed Governor of Worcester, but when the Duke of Hamilton raised his Scotch force, and entered England, he joined him, and escaped to Ireland after the battle of Winwick, where he joined the Duke of Ormond. The Irish officers became jealous of his leadership, and the Duke could not place him in any conspicuous command. After the Duke of Ormond's forces were defeated and scattered at Rathmines he fled to Scotland, and joined Prince Charles, and marched back to his native county with the Prince. He was left in Preston by the

Prince to raise a second force, while he went on to Worcester. The rest of his adventurous and courageous career has just been told. He died in the county which he loved so much, and in the cause of his King, and, like the noble Earl, as a loyal soldier, and was buried in the Tyldesley chapel in Leigh Parish Church. Major-General Sir William Witherington and Colonel Boynton were buried in the churchyard of Wigan.[1] Sir William Throckmorton was left for dead on the field, but an old woman discovered that he was alive, and with difficulty helped him to the house of Mr. Bradshaw, where he became a prisoner, together with Sir Timothy Featherston Haugh, and several other officers.

The horsemen fled with the Earl through Wigan on to Worcester, but that battle was

[1]Appendix Note VII.

as disastrous as Wigan for the Royalists. The description of the fighting does not come within the scope of this volume. All that need be said is that the young King escaped, and after an adventurous flight for forty-four days through the western counties and along the south coast he succeeded in finding a ship near Brighton, which landed him safely in France. The Scottish horse fled from the field with such speed that on the following day, Thursday, at three o'clock, they reached Sandbach, seventy miles off, where it being the market day, the townsmen and the country people attacked them with clubs and staves and the poles from their stalls. Another portion of the flying Scots, to the number of 500, passed over the ferry at Hollins Green, not daring to attempt the bridge at Warrington, which was in possession of the enemy, and kept against

H

them. These were met by a force in
command of Colonel Holcroft as they were
trying to make their way through Culcheth
to the north. A very sharp encounter took
place not far from Holcroft Hall itself, when
more than 100 were slain, and the rest taken
prisoners. The district where the dead
bodies were buried was afterwards called by
the inhabitants " bury loane," and to this day
one still hears that name given to the district
by the older residents of the township of
Culcheth.[1]

[1]Appendix Note VIII.

Part 1.

Chapter xi. The capture of the Earl of Derby—his petition to Cromwell—his escape from Chester Castle and recapture—Lord Strange's ride to London to the House of Commons—the last words of the Earl, and the scene of the execution.

The Romance of

Chief Characters: { Lord Derby. Lord Strange. } { Cromwell. Bradshaw. } Colonels Holcroft and Birch. Captain Sankey and Mr. Bridgeman

CHAPTER XI.

THE EARL OF DERBY also escaped at the battle of Worcester, and wandered about the country, until at last he, with a Scottish Lord, named Lauderdale, fell into the hands of Captain Edge, a Lancashire man, who took them prisoners, giving them quarter, and brought them to Chester. The Earl was imprisoned in the Castle, with a guard of soldiers to attend him.

The Parliament took no notice of the quarter given him, but commanded that the Earl, together with Sir Timothy Featherston

Haugh and Captain Benlowe, should be tried by court martial. They were sentenced to die. He was to be taken to Boulton to be beheaded. He, however, feeling he had not been dealt with fairly, after quarter had been given him, appeals to the Protector.

To the Right Honourable his Excellencie, the Lord Generall Cromwell.

The humble Petition of James, Earle of Derby, a Sentenced Prisoner in Chester, sheweth :—

That it appeareth by the annexed what plea your Petitioner hath urged for life, in which the Court Martiall here were pleased to over-rule him. It being a matter of Law, and a point not adjudged nor presidented in all this Warr ; and the plea being only capable of Appeale to your Excellencie's wisdom, which will safely resolve it, and your Petitioner being also a Prisoner to the High Court of

Parliament in relation to his Rendition of the Isle of Man.

> In all he most humbly craves your Excellencie's grace that he may as well obtain your Excellencie's judgment on his plea on the Parliament's mercy, with your Excellencie's favour to him, and he shall owe his life to your Lordship's service.
>
> And ever pray,
>
> DARBY.

The petition was not answered, at least not before he decided to make an attempt to escape from the Castle. His friends were allowed to communicate with him, and they arranged and successfully carried out his escape. His friends having furnished the rope, and thrown it up to him upon the Castle wall, he let himself down. He thus made good his escape. He was soon missed, however, and diligent search made for him, but he was some distance from the city before he was captured, and brought back to the Castle, when he was more strictly guarded.

His execution was hurried forward, and the sentence was to be carried out by October the 15th.

Finding that Parliament was determined not to answer Lord Derby's petition, Lord Strange, the eldest son of Lord Derby, who had remained neutral for some cause during the Civil Wars, and had resided quietly at Knowsley, rode with all speed to London to get the petition read in the House, hoping that his neutrality during the Wars would have influence with the members. Mr. Lenthall, the Speaker, received the petition favourably, but when Cromwell and Bradshaw saw that the greater part of the House were inclined to allow the Earl's plea (as the

Speaker was putting the question), they, with
some eight or nine others, left the House, so
that the number left was under forty, no
question could therefore be put. Lord
Strange seeing that all efforts to save his
father had failed, and that Cromwell had
determined that he should die, rode back
hastily to see his father before his execution.
He arrived a few hours before the time, and
his father affectionately embracing him said,
"Son, I thank you for your duty, diligence,
and best endeavours to save my life! but
since it cannot be obtained, I must submit,"
and kneeling down, he said, "Domine, non
mea voluntas sed Tua."

The scene of the execution was a memor-
able one. The Earl was much beloved
throughout the county, and he had the sympathy of even his opponents. Two regiments
of Colonel Jones', and commanded by

Captain Sankey, were ordered to convey him from Chester to Bolton. They started on the 13th October, Monday. As they passed through Warrington the crowds gazed on the solemn procession with tearful eyes, and numbers joined the procession to follow the noble Earl to his place of execution. Journeying along through Winwick, Newton, and Lowton, Captain Sankey was joined by Colonel Holcroft and Thomas, and other gentlemen of the neighbourhood. At Leigh, where he was allowed to rest, the crowd was further increased by Colonel Birch and a vast number from the Manchester side. Many thousands spent that night and the following one in Bolton, waiting for the execution on Wednesday, the 15th, at 2 p.m.

A scaffold had been erected not far from the Old Market Cross, supposed to be the very place, or near to the place, where he slew Captain Bootle (an old servant, who had taken up arms on the Parliamentary side), which accusation he stoutly denied on the scaffold.

When coming to the foot of the ladder to go up to the scaffold he kissed it, saying : "I am thus requited for my love. I submit to the will of God." And having ascended the scaffold, he began to speak to the people as follows :—

" Good Christians :

" Since it hath pleased God thus to take away my life, I am glad it must be in this Town, where some have been made to believe I am a man of blood. It is a slander that I should be the death of any. It was my desire, the last time I was in the county, to come hither as to a people that ought to serve the King, and (as I conceive) upon good grounds. Whereas it was said I was accustomed to be a man of blood. It doth not lie upon my conscience, for I am wrongfully belied, being one that desired Peace.

"I was born in honour, having lived in honour, and hope I shall die with honour. I had a fair estate, and needed not to mend that. I had friends, by whom I was respected, and I respected them. They were ready to do for me, and I was ready to do for them. I have done nothing but after the example of my predecessors to do you good. It was the King that called me in, and I thought I was bound to wait upon him to do him service."

At that moment the crowd was moved to a tumult, many weeping and crying, "He is innocent. It is a shame for the Earl to die." It was some time before the crowd ceased to shout, and when the uproar had

subsided he looked around him, and said:
"I thought to have spoken more, but I
have done, and I shall not enlarge anything,
save only my good will to this town of
Bolton. I put my trust in Jesus Christ."
And once more looking on every side, he
said: "I never deserved this from above;
and as for you, honest friends that are
soldiers, you know that my life is taken from
me after that quarter was given me, and that
by a Council of War, which was never done
before to any."

He then walked to and fro upon the
scaffold, with his head bent upon his breast,
speaking to himself, while the crowd in deep
sympathy wept aloud. Hearing their wailing,
he suddenly stood still, and gazing at the
masses of weeping faces before him and
around him, he said: "The Lord bless you
all. The Son of God Almighty bless you

all of this town of Bolton, Manchester, and all Lancashire. God send you a King again. I die here a soldier, a Christian soldier."

He then sat down in the chair which had been provided for him, and, turning to the soldier nearest to him, said : "They are not ready yet," for the block had not been prepared. He then asked the soldier "to commend him to all his good friends in Chester, and to tell them that he died like a soldier."

He also asked for his coffin to be brought which was to convey his body to his burial place. It was placed upon the scaffold, and after it had been opened, he said : "When I lie imprisoned here, a guard will not need to attend me with swords." The people, hearing his words, groaned and wailed again. After a brief interval, as he watched the preparations for his execution, he once more rose from his chair, and again walking up and down the scaffold, and looking around, he said : "There is not one man that revileth me, God be thanked." And, turning round to those who stood with him on the scaffold, he said : "What do you stay for ? It is hard I cannot get a block to have my head cut off." Casting his eye upon the executioner, he said to him : "Thy coat is so burly, thou wilt never hit aright. The Lord bless thee and forgive thee." Then, speaking to Mr. Bridgeman, he said : "They have brought me hither too soon. The block is not ready for me. Mr. Bridgeman, tell your brother I take it a great mercy of God that I am brought hither, for I might have died in the midst of a battle, and not died so well, for now I have had time to make my peace with God."

He then requested his servant to lay his

head on the block to see how it would fit;
but on his refusal, the trumpeter who was
standing by laid his neck upon it to try. The
Earl then knelt down, and laid his neck
upon the block, and raising it again, he asked
that the block might be turned. Then,
laying his neck upon it again, he said:
"Do not strike yet." After a few seconds,
he raised himself up, and paced up and down
on the scaffold, saying: "Good people, I
desire your prayers; I desire your prayers.
I pray God bless you. The Son of God
bless you all. The Lord bless this nation.
And the Lord bless my poor wife and
children." For a few minutes there was
intense silence throughout the crowd, as the
Earl knelt in quiet prayer. He then laid
his head upon the block, saying to the
executioner: "When I lift up my hand, give
me the blow." But, just as he gave the

sign, one of his servants that stood by stepped forward, and said : "My Lord, let me speak with you before——" Whereupon the Earl looked up, and when the conversation ended he turned to the executioner, and said : "I have given you the sign, and it was ill mist." Then, still upon his knees, he said, as he faced the people : "Honest friends, I thank God I neither fear man nor death. I rejoice to serve the King and my country. I am sorry to leave so many of my friends ; but I hope the Lord will keep and bless them. The Lord of Heaven bless my poor wife and children. The Lord bless His people and my good King. Blessed be God's name for ever and ever. Amen. And let all the earth be filled with His glory." Then, giving the last sign by lifting his hand, the executioner raised his axe, when a piercing cry and yell came from the women as they hid their faces in their kerchiefs, whilst his head was severed from his body with one blow. His servants quickly lifted the severed head and body, and joined them together again as they placed the remains in the coffin there ready. The same night his body was carried to Ormskirk to rest with his ancestors.

Colonel Blood.

Part 1.

Chapter xii. The marriage of Thomas Holcroft and Eleanor Birch —a sketch of the life of Colonel Birch—Maria's return with her husband to Ireland.

The Romance of

Chief Characters: COLONEL BIRCH.
THOMAS HOLCROFT AND ELEANOR
BIRCH.
COLONEL BLOOD AND MARIA.

Colonel Blood.

CHAPTER XII.

ON August 31st, 1652, Thomas Holcroft
and Eleanor Birch, the daughter of Colonel
Birch, were married. [1]

Colonel Birch (with Colonel Holcroft) had
joined the Parliamentary forces early in 1642.
They entered Manchester with a small force,
and beat to arms in the same year. At the
house of Mr. Greene were Lord Strange,
Thomas Tyldesley, and others, who, after a
shot or two were fired from the window, left

[1] Thomas Holcroft et Eleanor Birch matrimonio copulati,
31st August, 1652.—Newchurch Parish Registers.

the banquet table, and entered into a sharp skirmish, in which Colonel Birch fled, it is said, under a cart, and was afterwards known under the nickname, the "carter."

Not more than a few weeks after this skirmish he, with Colonel Harrison, was imprisoned for opposing the Lathom lay. He was soon, however, released, and in the same year was made a Major in Colonel Assheton's regiment, and in March of the year 1643 Lord Fairfax made him Colonel of a foot regiment. He took part in nearly all the engagements in the county, and in 1644 was appointed Governor of Liverpool. In 1646 he was in Gloucestershire, commanding a regiment under Sir Wm. Brereton, and defeated Sir Jacob Astley's forces at Stow-en-the-Wold. In 1649, just after the battle of Winwick, he was elected M.P. for Liverpool, on the death of Sir Richard

Colonel Blood.

Wynn. At the battle of Wigan-lane his
company became conspicuous, with Colonel
Holcroft's, in the slaughter of the Earl's foot
regiments, of which the reader is already
familiar. He had also taken part in the
storming of Lathom House, and assisted at
the reduction of the Isle of Man, the Ladies
Stanley being placed under his charge. In
1654 and 1656 he was again returned as
M.P. for Liverpool, and in 1659 he was
fighting again when Sir George Booth was
routed at Winnington. He recklessly removed some of the old muniments from the
old Parish Church of Manchester to London,
where they were unfortunately destroyed by
fire. In 1660, in Parliament, Sir Ralph
Assheton informed the House that a person
who had sat in the last Parliament took a
bond for £100 for some particular service
done in the House, and when asked to name

the person he gave the name of Colonel Thomas Birch, of Liverpool. He lived to a good old age, outliving his neighbour, Thomas Holcroft, by fifteen years, and died in 1678, age 71.

The words of the Rev. William Leigh had come true (except for the time), and true to his word his reverence tasted the finest port that he had ever drunk as he toasted the bride and bridegroom in Holcroft Hall, for he was spared to officiate, but the event which was solemnised on that day was with different surroundings than those of June 21st, 1650. The church was full of wedding guests. All was bright, and the gathered assembly were full of congratulations for the happy pair.

By this time the bitter feeling against the marriage of Colonel Blood and Maria had worn itself out. Blood was received into that select county gathering as a gallant and successful officer, and one who had a brilliant career before him. He was a man of courtly manners, affable and witty, and on this occasion was the most interesting person of the honoured guests. This was the proudest day of Maria's married life. All family feuds were ended, and her husband was respected, admired and flattered by those who but two years ago had looked with disdain, and spoken with horror of the marriage with the unknown adventurer.

Colonel Blood took back his wife and child. It was a new experience for Maria, but having a determined mind, she settled down to her life as she made acquaintance with her husband's friends. An estate had been portioned out to him, the sequestered or confiscated property of some poor soul who had been killed or sent as a prisoner to

Barbadoes. And there in Dublin Maria entered into that strange and eventful work of a Parliamentary officer's household, which was oftentimes the meeting place of the notorious, wicked, and treacherous characters of a country which never remained free for any great length of time from intrigue and cruel and horrible crime.

Colonel Blood.

Part 1.

Chapter xiii. The Irish Acts of Settlement after its subjugation —Fleetwood's hatred of the Irish — Henry Cromwell sent as a peace-maker, and Fleetwood's retirement — Colonel Blood and the meeting of the "Tories" —the Baptists.

The Romance of

Chief Characters: THE LORD DEPUTY FLEETWOOD.
HENRY CROMWELL AND COLONEL
BLOOD.

CHAPTER XIII.

WHILE Cromwell was troubled with his
Parliaments in England, while plots against
his person were being laid and revealed, and
his whole time seemed occupied in dissolving
one and executing the authors of the other,
Ireland was being dealt with in a most harsh
and cruel manner. The settlement of Ireland
after its devastation was no easy matter.
Thousands escaped the heavy penalties im-
posed upon the inhabitants by emigration.
Indeed Cromwell was of the opinion that
" Ireland could only be brought within the
pale of civilisation by a majority of English

hands and brains." Emigration was encouraged by the merciless Acts of Settlement, so that, at least, some 40,000 were banished. The settled belief of every Englishman in that day was that the massacre of 1641 cried aloud for punishment, if not for vengeance. Heavy taxes were laid upon those who were fortunate enough to remain in their native land, so that a writer has stated : "The tax swept away their whole substance ; necessity made them turn thieves and 'Tories,' and then they were persecuted with fire and sword for being so. If they discovered not Tories, the English hanged them ; if they did, the Irish killed them ; against whom they had nothing to defend themselves ; and if any person, melted with the bowels of a man, or moved by the rules of common equity, laboured to bring home to them that little mercy which the State allowed, there

were some ready to asperse them as favourers
of Tories, coverers of blood-guiltiness ; and
briefly, in a probable computation, five parts
of six of the whole nation were destroyed."
This may be exaggeration, yet certainly the
greater part of the country was lying waste
and desolate, and, according to Petty, one-
third of the Irish perished by the sword,
plague, famine, hardship, and banishment.
In 1653, Cromwell had assumed the Protectorate, and not feeling satisfied with the
government in Ireland, and hearing rumours
calling in question the fidelity of the army,
he sent his son, Henry, to ascertain the
truth, and bring back a report. Henry was
of a mediatory and conciliatory spirit, and
brought back a fairly satisfactory report, and
Fleetwood was appointed Lord Deputy.
But Fleetwood, who hated the Irish, was
determined to carry out the "work of

transplanting the Irish proprietors, and such as had been in arms" during the war, and wrote to Thurloe that "these people are an abominable, false, cunning, and perfidious people, and the best of them to be pitied, but not to be trusted." His conduct was not in accordance with Cromwell's wishes or Parliament's orders. Besides, he was constantly showering favours upon the Baptists that his patronage became notorious. The Baptists in England were of a rebellious character, and in Ireland they had become numerous and influential in the army, and this gave "umbrage to the Government, which had had experience of the revolutionary tendencies of many of their co-religionists in England."

Henry Cromwell was again sent as Major-General to command the army under Fleetwood, and Parliament thought that his conciliatory spirit would bring peace. He arrived in Ireland on July 9th, 1665. Fleetwood became defiant, but Henry's influence was strong, and "by the beginning of August, Fleetwood's retirement was common talk." "The crowd which had hitherto followed him in his attendance at the service of the Baptist[1] congregation now followed Henry Cromwell to the lately deserted 'public service' instituted by the instrument of Goverment. The Provost of Trinity hailed the son of the Proctector as the future ruler of the country." Fleetwood left Ireland in September, and Henry was appointed Deputy. Colonel Blood was then made a Commissioner of Parliament, and a more secular regime was introduced, and the Baptist officers, who had styled themselves "the godly," were no longer scandalously promoted. [1]Appendix Note IX.

K

But the Tories were of the greatest trouble to the Government; and to Blood was entrusted the work of capturing these outlaws. Being in command, and by virtue a magistrate, he could hold a court martial on the spot, and execute them before the eyes of the rest. But it was a long, weary work. Like the small band of Boers in the late Boer war, they lived in the open, and escaped capture from time to time, harassing the Government, till the most severe measures were taken against them.

Toree or Tory was the name given to these Irish outlaws, who infested the bogs and woods of Ireland. "They were of the wildest and hardiest of the native Irish who refused to submit to Enlgish yoke. Swooping down upon English settlers, and with still greater delight on the habitations of Irishmen who had submitted, they plundered and slew them to their hearts' delight. Fear, or reluctance to betray their countrymen, rendered the Irish peasant slow to give information which might lead to the capture of the marauders. To check the complicity of the natives, orders were given in Cork precincts that the Irish remaining in their old quarters should be collected in villages, in which at least thirty families were to be drawn together, and that these villages should not be within half a mile of wood, bog, or mountain. Care, too, was to be taken for the appointment of a headman, with the duty of bringing in the cattle every night, and setting watch over them. A few weeks later a party of Tories murdered an Irishman who served the English as a constable at Timolin. As the Tories were countenanced by the inhabitants of the neighbourhood, and no information was given, all the Irish Papists in Timolin were ordered to transplantation as a punishment, their cabins being burnt, and rates levied on the barony for the relief of the widow. Later on, perhaps in revenge for their punishment, another band of Tories swooped down on eight English surveyors at Timolin, carried them into the woods, and there murdered them. In vain prices were set on the heads of the leaders of the Tories. If some were brought in and hanged, others quickly slipped into their places. At last in January, 1655, the Government denounced the ingratitude of the Irish rebels, who, notwithstanding the mercy and favour of Parliament to all who would live peaceably under English rule, nevertheless continued in their evil courses, disturbing all who desired to live peaceably, by "murders, spoils, rapines, and thefts." The officers in each precinct were

therefore ordered to act as a court martial
to judge summarily in such cases. No quarter was any longer to be given. So the
renewed struggle was carried on in all its
horrors. Colonel Blood was ever searching
the mountains for these fearless Tories. He
was as fearless, daring, and bloodthirsty as
they were, and just the man to roam the
country to exterminate the lawless bands.
As they were caught they were either hanged
or sent as vagabonds to English colonies
beyond the sea—to New England, Virginia,
the West Indies, and especially Barbadoes,
to work like slaves on the plantations.

Part i.

The Romance of

Chief Characters:

HENRY CROMWELL AND COLONEL BLOOD.
GENERAL MONK AND PRINCE CHARLES.
DUKE OF ORMOND AND COLONEL BLOOD.
THOMAS RISLEY.

Colonel Blood.

CHAPTER XIV.

CROMWELL'S death in 1658 was a blow to the
Parliamentarians. The army came to the
fore, and as Blood was a believer in the
power of the army, he influenced Henry
Cromwell to acknowledge the Rump Parliament, which had been reinstated by the army
in England. But the rule of the army—a
rule by sword—was not one that could last
in England. The strange conduct of Richard
Cromwell, and the severe quarrels between
the army and Parliament, made the people
long for an hereditary head. Henry Cromwell's position in Ireland became insecure,
together with those officers who, like Blood,

had kept the Royalists at bay for over ten years. The Roman Catholic Royalists were most anxious to receive Prince Charles (whose views were known to be in sympathy with them), and would have hailed with delight his advent into Ireland. But England was preparing to receive him. Ireland was kept back from raising an army by the pressure of the iron rule from the Castle. General Monk had marched from Scotland, and gained possession of the power by his wonderful courage and tact. And, seeing the growing feeling of the people, secretly arranged with Charles for a messenger to come to England to make known his policy. When General Monk announced in Parliament that a messenger from Charles waited for admission the news was hailed with delight, and a warm invitation dispatched to the Prince, who returned to his native land.

Colonel Blood.

In May, 1660, Charles was proclaimed King Charles II. at the gate of Westminster Hall, and within a month he landed at Dover, and made his public entry into London on his birthday.

From this date Blood became the notorious and desperate character which has made his name so renowned for his daring exploits.

The Duke of Ormond was again appointed the Lord Lieutenant. Blood would not serve under him, and he became a rebel and a conspirator against the new rule and authorities at Dublin Castle. The Act of Settlement was the crisis. He was deprived of his estate, and dismissed from the army, and thus became a wandering fortune hunter, outlaw, and fearless desperado.

His wife, with her two children—the boy who was born in Culcheth, and a girl born in Ireland—he escorted safely to England,

and they once more landed at Culcheth, where for a time they resided at Holcroft Hall.

Thomas Holcroft's married life had been most happy. Eleanor Birch had made an excellent wife, and had borne three children — Eleanor, Margaret, and Alice. They lived quietly and happily, and it was a comfort to Maria to get back, and to rest from the turmoil of the life in Ireland, and to be free from the daily task of listening to the stories of intrigue and crime. Eleanor was also delighted to see her old friend once more and her children in her native country and her old home.

While the reader is brought back again to Culcheth it will be interesting to him to have a short sketch of the career of Thomas

Risley, who had been robbed of the love of Maria by Colonel Blood.

After entering Pembroke College, Oxford, he in time became a Fellow of his College, and his assiduity and his abilities earned for himself no mean reputation. On the 10th November, 1662, he was ordained simultaneously a Deacon and Priest by the Bishop of Norwich. But in the same year the act of Uniformity[1] was passed, to the terms of which he could not conscientiously comply, which thus forced him to resign his Fellowship. He was held in such high esteem by his College that they allowed him twelve months for deliberation. This deliberation was guided by the training and the warning of his father in his early days, and he therefore decided not to conform. He thus forfeited his Fellowship, and formed one of the number

[1] Appendix Note X.

whom the act ejected from their livings in the Church.

From his chair in the University he retired to his estate in Risley. There he ministered privately to such of his neighbours as coincided with him. For the sake of being of service to the sick poor he commenced the study of medicine. About four years after his retirement he received from the Vice-Chancellor of the University a pressing invitation to return, with a promise of immediate preferment on condition that he conformed. The way thus opened might have tempted one of less liberal views, but he could not satisfy his mind regarding the subscriptions required. He therefore declined the proferred favour, and remained in Risley, where, forgetting Maria Holcroft, he married, and settled on his estate, and became the neighbour of Thomas Holcroft. He was not free, however, from persecutions. Accusations were levelled not only against Presbyterians, but also against many worthy ministers on charges of rioting and of plotting against the Sovereign. Thomas Risley had to leave his family until the Act of Toleration. He then returned, built a meeting house[1] under the five mile Act[2] and formed a regular congregation, and ministered to them until his death, in 1715, at the age of 86, his son, John Risley, taking up the charge.

[1] Appendix Note XI.
[2] Appendix Note XII.

Part ii.

The Adventures

Chief Characters: General Ludlow.
Colonel Jones.
Lord Chancellor Steele.
Colonel Blood and Brother
Officers.

CHAPTER XV.

IN 1659, in the Protectorate of Richard Cromwell, a Colonel Jones was sent over to Ireland, and made one of the Commissioners with General Ludlow, the Commander-in-Chief of the Forces, and one of his colleagues. Colonel Jones knew Ireland well. He had been sent as one of the Commissioners in 1647. He was of a very pious disposition, and began his reforms by correcting abuses in the brewing of ale, and even excluded from any public office any person who was known to frequent a tavern. He had fought against the Duke of Ormond, and routed his army, which led to the surrender of Dublin to Parliament; and completely demoralised the forces of Lord Preston at Trim, when some 6,000 were killed and taken prisoners. He had fought side by side with Blood when Cromwell went in 1649, and returned with him in 1650, after his terrible slaughter and havoc. While in England he was sent to guard the Earl of Derby on his way to Chester, through Warrington and Leigh, to Bolton, and was present at the Earl's execution on October 15th, 1651. He was in high favour with Cromwell, whose widowed sister, Catherine, he married, and he was made one of his lords in 1657, receiving from Parliament in reward for his services in Ireland a grant of land and £3,000.

of Colonel Blood.

At the time when Colonel Blood seized him, and confined him in the Castle, there was much discontent in the Irish Government, and more prominence was given to Jones than the Irishmen liked. It may be that he was reserved, and had little dealings with the rather reckless characters of his less Puritanical brother officers. He was so pious that even in those days he was called by his own troops a religious fanatic, and, like Cromwell, prayed with his mouth while he killed with his hand.

General Ludlow, knowing Colonel Jones's trustworthiness, and his skill in commanding, and not heeding the general feeling of dislike to his rule, returned to England, and left him as his deputy. This was too much for Blood and his brother officers. Even Lord Chancellor Steele would not serve with him, and departed for England. Thus for the time being the whole of the government was in his hands. But an incident occurred which Blood took advantage of, and was thus able to carry out his plot to make Jones a prisoner, and prevent him using his power, which was so disliked.

Lambert, the Commander of the English force, had quarrelled with the Rump Parliament after he had put down the insurrection which had broken out in Cheshire, and the Parliament was for a second time ejected. This was Blood's opportunity. He sowed the seeds of discontent amongst his brother officers of the army, and believing that they had now the upper hand, they successfully carried out the plot. They first seized Colonel Jones, and then captured the Castle, and took the reins of Government out of his hands. Blood was really doing in Dublin what Lambert was doing in London. Having now the power, the Army declared for a Free Parliament, and kept Colonel Jones a close prisoner. But this power was not to last long. Lambert was defeated by General Monk from Scotland, and the Army, distrusting its leaders, began to make terms once more with the Parliament they had just recently ejected, so that on December 26th, 1659, the Rump Parliament was reinstated. Colonel Jones was commanded to be released, and immediately proceeded to England, where Parliament thought he might be of great use. But the arrival of General Monk in London changed all their plans. The Rump Parliament was dissolved, and by April 26th, 1660, a new Parliament had been elected. For some time Jones concealed himself, but he was at last detected in Finsbury, and made a prisoner, and sent to the Tower. He was brought to trial on the

12th October, being charged, with others, in the share they had in the execution of King Charles I. His last words on the scaffold at Charing Cross were words of admirable fortitude and resignation. "It was the power that made the law," he said, "for that some years before he and his party had the power in their hands, and whatsoever they did at that time was accounted law, and executed accordingly. Now that the King executed the law upon them, he did nothing but what he would have done himself were he in the King's case ; for that the King did but act like a loving and dutiful son towards a dear and loving father !" He then said "he was free from any charge of malice against the late King," and kneeling down in prayer, he calmly and reverently submitted to the executioner's axe.

Part ii.

Chapter xvi. The reason of Blood's hatred of the Duke of Ormond—his strange plot to capture the Duke — the plot revealed and the capture of seven M.P.'s—the scene of the execution, and the report of the coming of Colonel Blood to rescue them — his escape to the mountains.

The Adventures

Chief Characters: THE DUKE OF ORMOND.
Mr. LECKIE.
COLONEL BLOOD.

CHAPTER XVI.

Colonel Blood's hatred of the Duke of Ormond was not new. He had fought against him in the days of Cromwell, and he believed him to be an enemy of liberty and justice. So bitter was his hatred that he decided to raise an insurrection, and, if possible, place himself at the head of the gathered forces and capture the Duke, and take possession of the Castle. He called upon all Protestants to take up arms against the King, and to fight for liberty. He posed as a pious Covenanter, and drew up a declaration for the people to sign, asking for the restoration of the Solemn League and Covenant. He gathered together in Dublin a great number of his fellow-comrades—discharged soldiers of the old Army—and revealed to them the plot for the taking of the Castle and the capture of the Duke. Among the number were men of good standing in the eyes of the Royalists, who were then sitting in the Irish Parliament. His own brother-in-law, who had given his allegiance to the King, was drawn into it, and was afterwards executed. Blood was no longer a soldier, and as a civilian he lays his plans. He selected six to gain admission into the Castle by carrying petitions on a pretence of presenting them to the Lord Lieutenant, while a contingent of about 100 men were to remain outside in ordinary civilian's clothing, ready to rush in as soon as the signal was given. The guards were to be put off their guard by a feigned accident on the part of a pretended baker, who was to carry a large basket of bread upon his shoulder. He was to stumble, upset his basket, and assume to be hurt, and thus put the guards in disorder. That was to be the signal to those inside the Castle and those outside. The guards were to be disarmed, and made prisoners by those outside, and the others were to secure the Duke and take possession of the Castle. This elaborate plot was not successful. Within his army of conspirators there were traitors. The plot was revealed to the Duke, and during the night soldiers were dispatched to the place of secret meeting, and many seized, among them being seven members of Parliament. Blood escaped; how! no one knows. It may be that they feared to take him, for his name was as much dreaded as Cromwell's. His brother-in-law, Leckie, one of the members of the Irish Parliament, together with others in this conspiracy, was condemned to be executed. Blood resolved to release them. It was a foolish attempt, and, like his plot, failed. Yet so much did they fear his name that on the morning of the execution, when the rumour spread that Blood was coming with an army to rescue them, they fled from the scene of the execution. Had Blood been there when the false alarm was given by the crowd, who shouted, " Blood, the divil, is coming " (for they said " the viry divil was in him "), he might have rescued them ; for on hearing the shout of the crowd the guards ran here and there, and even the executioner left his place by the side of the condemned, leaving the rope upon his neck. Blood did

of Colonel Blood.

not arrive in time. His army was met
outside the city, and driven, after a desperate
and fierce fight, to the mountains. For
some months he was hiding among the hills,
and at last escaped by way of Scotland, where
the fierce persecutions were being carried
on with relentless cruelty by Middleton,
Lauderdale, and Sharpe.[1] The One Mile
Act,[2] passed, it is said, by a drunken Parliament, had just been introduced, which was
very severe upon the Covenanters. A
rivalry had arisen between Middleton[3] and
Lauderdale,[4] in which Lauderdale gained the
mastery, so that Middleton was removed, and
Lauderdale became the Chief Commissioner,
which in no sense abated the persecution.

[1] Appendix Note XIII.   [3] Appendix Note XV.
[2] Appendix Note XIV.   [4] Appendix Note XVI.

Part ii.

Chapter xvii. General Monk's march from Scotland — his defeat of General Lambert—entrance into London — joy of the people—his negotiations with Charles II.—his tact in preserving peace—the crowning of Charles II. — Colonel Blood's plot to kill General Monk during the great plague — its discovery — the two traitors—trial and pardon.

The Adventures

Chief Characters: GENERALS MONK AND LAMBERT.
CHARLES II.
THE DUKES OF ORMOND AND
CLARENDON.
COLONEL BLOOD AND TRAITORS.

CHAPTER XVII.

IF ever there was a man wanted with a firm and determined courage, and yet at the same time with a willingness to adapt himself to the course events would take, it was in the year 1660. It needed a man "as wise as a serpent, and as harmless as a dove," or a man to act in that character. A man was found—a man respected by his troopers, and a most successful officer—General Monk. For many years he had been in command in Scotland during the Protectorate, and when the English army was divided in its allegiance, some being

175

favourable to Parliamentary control, and others having faith only in the power of the army itself, Monk came forward, and by wonderful tact and boldness saved the country from what was gradually growing into another civil war. On December 8th, 1659, he crossed the Tweed with over 7,000 men, and defeated Lambert (the head of the English army), who had marched to Newcastle to oppose his advance, and took him prisoner. Monk on his march to London was able to ascertain the feeling of the people, and found that they were in favour of a free Parliament. The Rump Parliament were, however deceived in him, thinking he was favourable to it, and under its orders he gained an entrance into the city. No sooner had he entered London than he declared himself favourable to a new Parliament. The people hailed with delight his decision. The joy in London was unbounded. Bonfires were lighted, oxen roasted, and the people marched in procession, with torches and rumps tied upon poles, to show their hatred of that Parliament.

General Monk demanded the restoration of the excluded Presbyterian members of Parliament, and under his wise advice the present Parliament dissolved itself, and issued writs for an election. Contrary to expectation, though the people had tired of the unsettled condition of the country and the continual strife between the army and Parliament, the new members of the House were most favourable to the Royal family. Monk, now being the head of the army, and adviser of Parliament, decided secretly to negotiate with Charles, and to state the conditions upon which he would be gladly received in London. Unfortunately Charles was ruled by the Duke of Ormond and others, and drew up a declaration at Breda, in which he promised almost all the conditions asked for, but with this proviso, that he would be advised by Parliament as to the terms he would give to the late Protector's army. The army, knowing the fickleness of Parliament, strongly resented this, and it will ever remain to General Monk's credit that by his marvellous tact, firmness, courage, and persuasion he put out the kindling fires of discontent. He organised what we now call the militia, to oppose the army, if by chance it determined not to receive Charles's terms.

The whole country was ready and willing to receive the King, except the army, but by General Monk's good sense and firmness the danger passed, and Charles was received with joy. Never had there been such joy.

Flowers were strewn along the road, the bells rang, and the old cavaliers who had fought at Edgehill, Naseby, and other sad battlefields, wept for joy, while the troopers of the Protector stood on Blackheath sad and angry.

General Monk strongly urged lenient treatment to the late Parliamentary forces, but the Duke of Ormond, the Earl of Clarendon, with other of the Royalists now in favour, meted out scanty pardon to them, being bent on restoring the property and the temporal power of those who had been favourable to the Royalists. It was this which made Colonel Blood so bitter against the Duke of Ormond, who, when Lord Lieutenant of Ireland, had dismissed him, and confiscated his property, so that practically he was reduced to poverty. Having escaped after his attempt on the Duke's life,

he arrived in London, only further to con-
spire and plot against General Monk. The
change of attitude of the General from a
Parliamentarian to a Royalist, and the
growing power of the General, who had now
been made Duke of Albermarle, gave Blood
an opportunity for revenge. If he could
not take Dublin Castle and the Duke of
Ormond, he would take the Tower, and
General Monk. He had become the leader
of a revolutionary party, which met in
defiance of Parliament, which party was
made up of every conceivable fanatic of the
times. As it was said of David when he
was hiding from Saul: "Everyone that was
in distress, and everyone that was in debt,
and everyone that was discontented, gathered
themselves unto him, and he became a
captain over them,"[1] so it could be said of
Blood.

[1] I Samuel, xxii. 2.

of Colonel Blood.

It was during the sad and terrible pestilence of the Black Plague, which swept like a hurricane over London, when over a hundred thousand fell victims to its awful ravages, that Blood timed this plot for the killing of the General and the taking of the Tower. London was deserted. The rich fled in terror. Charles and his Court removed to Oxford. Few noblemen were brave enough to share the misery of the poor souls who had no chance of quitting the city. But General Monk once more showed his courage and his devotion to the people by remaining in the city, and going in and out among the plague-stricken crowd, ministering to the wants and necessities of the dying, protecting the property of the absent ones, and keeping order in a city so full of disease, crime, and outrage. Blood had no lack of ingenuity in every plot that he made, and his plans were most cleverly laid, yet the boldness of them was only equalled by their foolishness. As in the first venture he found traitors among his accomplices, so in this second plot, he finds that there are traitors amongst traitors, as well as thieves among thieves. He heard that the reports of their meetings were being constantly carried to the General. It was most difficult to detect the culprits, and not until the final meeting to arrange the day for the attack were the culprits detected. On that evening two of whom they had had suspicion absented themselves, and thus revealed who were the traitors, and that night the soldiers entered the premises, and captured, among others, Colonel John Rathbone and Captain Mason, while some fled to Holland, and others to Scotland. Blood again escaped, but before he left

of Colonel Blood.

London he arranged a meeting with the two traitors at an inn in the city, where he seized them, and carried them off to a hired room, where a mock trial was held. They were found guilty, and condemned to be shot as traitors. They were then bound, and kept in the room for two days, when they were brought out, and led into the country. Their hands were bound behind them, their breasts bared, and the executioners commanded to present pistols. At this point Blood delivered this oration : "Thomas Faithless and William Coward, ye stand ready to receive the sentence of the law. Ye have been guilty of a crime cowardly and ignominious. To betray a trust, be it good or ill, is the act of a traitor. Ye were received in good faith by the Council, and false knaves that ye are, ye made known the plot, in which ye yourselves were assentors.

Ye have escaped the plague ; ye shall not escape the just punishment of your cowardly act. Hell hath received thousands of your vile brethren these two months. Go ye to them, for ye shall not live." Then, raising his arm as if to give the signal for their death, he said : "Have ye aught to say ere I command your executioners to fire ?" The men, expecting no mercy from so hardened and angry a judge, said : "Pray grant us mercy. We swear we will never betray thy name."

"Ye lie, ye cowards, ye have already revealed it. And for £100 ye agreed to guide to my capture. Take now your rewards, ye cowards," said Blood, as he unbound their hands, and gave them each a paper, on which was written :

"Pardoned."

T. Blood.

184

of Colonel Blood.

and said : "Go tell His Grace what has happened, and pray him to be as merciful to those whom he has captured as I have been to you." If the two men carried the message to His Grace, the Duke of Albermarle's mercy was not shown, for in April, 1666, Colonel Rathbone, with others, was tried at the Old Bailey, and condemned.

Part ii.

Chapter xviii. Colonel Blood joins the Covenanters in Scotland—the instrument of torture called the 'boot' —he escapes to Ireland, but is hunted out—returns to London —rescues Captain Mason near Doncaster— the scene at the Inn—the fight—his escape to Holland.

The Adventures

Part II.

Chief Characters: COLONEL BLOOD.
LORD DUNGANNON.
CAPTAIN MASON.
THE GUARD.

CHAPTER XVIII.

"The rescuing from justice of Captain Mason,
   Whom all the world doth know t' have been a base one."

Elegy on Colonel Blood (Brit. Mus.)

COLONEL BLOOD fled to Scotland, and joined the Covenanters. Scotland at this time was suffering from the oppression exercised by Sir John Turner. From the first year of Charles II. they had been bitterly persecuted, and after the execution of the Duke of Argyle, Johnson, and Guthrie, the Covenanters were ever rising against the hard and unfair measures which were being passed against them. Meetings for worship were held in the open air, and were called

189   N

Conventicles, to which the worshippers came, not with bibles only, but with swords and pistols. The King and his advisers were determined to uproot Presbyterianism, and establish Episcopacy. Sharp, a Presbyterian minister, and the Earl of Lauderdale betrayed the covenanters, and joined the cause of Episcopacy. Sharp was made Archbishop of St. Andrew's, and Lauderdale was made Chief Commissioner. With harsh and cruel measures the renegades persecuted their stauncher brethren, and even resorted to the ways of the Inquisition. One of the more terrible and infamous instruments of torture was called the "boot." It was made of four pieces of board, hooped with iron, and was placed upon the leg of the faithful Covenanter, while wedges were driven with a mallet between the flesh and the wood, until the whole limb, flesh and bone, was often crushed to an unsightly and horrible mass.

The severe measures of oppression in the Western Lowlands excited the stern Covenanters to insurrection again, and Colonel Blood joined them at Kirkcudbright. They marched on successfully, and advanced towards Edinburgh, but were defeated by General Dalziel at Rullion Green, near the Pentland Hills. Many executions followed, and fresh oppression started. Blood escaped, and fled to Ireland, but no sooner was his presence known there than reports of an extraordinary character were circulated. "He had come back to avenge the execution of his brother-in-law," they said, and the report spread from county to county. In Dublin the authorities were terribly alarmed, for they feared his presence among them. They imagined he would make another attempt on the castle and the person of the Duke of Ormond. Ulster was his hunting ground. There were more Protestants there than any other province of Ireland, but the Earl of Dungannon was a match for him, and hunted him from town to mountain, and mountain to port, from whence he once more escaped.

The ravages of the terrible plague were over in London, and the Great Fire had thoroughly cleansed the city by the removal of many of the black spots and filthy narrow streets in which it was still lingering, when Colonel Blood next visited London. Having settled in Romford as an apothecary, he sent for Maria and her two children from Culcheth, where he lived unsuspected and unmolested. But the spirit of intrigue and adventure was ever uppermost, and there needed little to move him to crime or bloodshed. He soon gathered around him his old associates, who had returned from Scotland or Holland, or who had escaped the plague and fire. Captain Mason, one of the conspirators in the plot to kill General Monk and take the Tower, had been detained in prison until the plot had been almost forgotten. He was, however, secretly dispatched with a guard of eight soldiers to the North, probably Durham, to await his trial at the Assizes. Colonel Blood having ascertained, by some secret method of inquiry, the route of the journey the guards were to take, decided if possible to rescue him. Having, therefore, chosen his confederates, they started, well prepared for the journey, on horseback, and their pistols hid away, and in the evening, to avoid suspicion. They rode for some days before they heard or saw anything of the prisoner and his escort. At

Newark, where they rested some time, thinking they had missed them, his confederates were for turning back, and giving up pursuit. But Blood was not a man to give up so easily, and after an exhortation and a threat, they were urged to go on. For two days they rode further, when towards evening of the second day they met with a convenient inn near to the town of Doncaster, and resolved to rest there that night, and if no news of the prisoner could be heard of they would return to London. They had not rested long when the sound of horses' feet attracted their attention. It was the guard with its prisoner stopping to take refreshment. Captain Mason was acting the generous by treating his guard with liquor. Finding the convoy was not staying the night at the inn, Blood stole out to the stables to prepare for following them, and to consider his plans for dealing with the eight guards. He had but three confederates, and how to tackle eight without a desperate struggle and without loss of life was a matter which needed skilful strategy. The marching of the guard helped him in his plans. He saw Captain Mason, on a disgraceful nag, start off with the Captain of the guard and four others. The others remained at the inn for some time, when one of the guards started off, leaving the last two drinking. Blood's confederates added liquor to liquor with these two, so that when they started off they were well nigh drunk. He then revealed his plans to his confederates, and throwing down the money in lieu of the night's rest, he excused himself and his friends by saying that they had found such good company that they had decided to go on their journey. His plans were that he and another should follow the last two guards, and, if possible, disable them, and then ride on to the single guardsman, and dispatch him. His other two confederates were to follow, and make sure that all was safe, and come on to their assistance to attack the five guardsmen. Blood and his companion, therefore, rode on, and soon overtook the last two guards.

"Good even, comrades, have ye ridden far?" said Blood, for he had not been seen by any of the guards.

"I warrant we have, for it is now six days since we left London," replied one of the guards.

"Ye be weary of your journey, I wager. What brings you this way?" questioned Blood.

"We have that bloodhound, Captain Mason, who with that devil of a Blood, has been plotting to kill the Duke of Albermarle," replied the guard.

196

"Has the Government not yet caught Blood, then?" inquired Blood.

"No; I wish the villain were caught. I would give a crown piece to know where the devil is," said the guard.

"Have they no thought of his hiding place, or whether he be in the country or no?" questioned Blood.

"No, I wager they would give £1,000 to the man who captured him," replied the guard.

"I would not give a thousand pence," said Blood, and his confederate coming up at that moment, he caught the bridle of one, and dismounted him, while his confederate did the same to the other. Fearing lest a shot might attract the attention of those on in front, they took the bridles from the horses, and let them wander away. Having thus made sure of these two, they rode on, hoping easily to dispatch the single rider, but they found he had joined the guards in front. Blood, in one of his mad and foolish ventures, galloped past them, and wheeling round, commanded them to halt. One of the guards, thinking he was drunk or mad, struck him with a switch, saying, " Fool, what dost thou mean ? Take that, and get thee on."

Blood returned the blow, and said, " Fool, what dost thou mean ? Take that, and get thee from thy saddle, ere I hurl thee to the ground."

He was now joined by his confederate, and in a few moments a good many blows had been exchanged. Captain Mason quietly rode on thinking it was but a drunken quarrel, and that his guards would soon follow. For some time they fought without drawing swords or pistols, but when Blood's other confederates joined him, a fierce and terrible struggle followed with pistol and sword. Captain Mason, hearing the report of arms, turned back, and finding that a severe fight was going on, and detecting Blood's voice shouting "Horse, horse quickly," he dismounted from his old nag, and jumped upon one of the now unmounted horses, and, without sword or pistol, threw himself into the fight. Blood was three times unhorsed owing to the neglect, in his hurry to get away from the inn, to regirth his saddle. At last he was so wounded that he could not remount, and two of the guards taking advantage of it, drove him against a wall, where he stood, with sword in one hand, and pistol in the other.

"Come on, ye cowards," growled Blood, mad with rage. And in return he received a shot in the shoulder, which made him drop his pistol. As he stood with his sword shielding his body, one of the two guards threw his discharged pistol at him, saying, "Thou art a devil, thou wilt never die." The pistol hit him between the eyes, and stunned him for a moment, and made him reel. He, however, raised himself up, and aimed a blow at his enemy with such force, saying, "But thou shalt die," that it brought the guard to the ground. Again he raised his sword and was about to deal to the other a similar blow, when Captain Mason, seeing who it was that was being smitten, stopped the stroke, saying, "Pray stay thy hand, this fellow hath shewn kindness to me along the way."

"That I will," replied Blood, "for I have no more strength left."

For two hours or more they had fought. Two of the guards were killed, besides a barber from York, who had joined them.

of Colonel Blood.

The rest were disabled, and Captain Mason was released. Blood had received five pistol wounds, besides being bruised from head to foot, and it was with great difficulty that they were able to get him away from the scene of so desperate an encounter. Blood, knowing somewhat of medicine, was able to instruct his comrades in attending his wounds, and by morning they were miles away, and had escaped. For some time they hid from justice in the famous hiding place of Robin Hood, Sherwood Forest, where they remained until quite convalescent, and then fled to Holland.

Part ii.

Chapter xix. Colonel Blood joins De Witt and De Ruyter and sails up the Thames—his return to Warrington under an assumed name — the quarrel between Richard Cavelveley and Hamlet Holcroft — Blood's return to London under the name Ayliffe—he practises as a physician — the seizing of the Duke of Ormond — his escape from justice.

The Adventures

CHAPTER XIX.

"The next ill thing he boldly undertook
Was barbarously seizing of a Duke."

Elegy on Colonel Blood (Brit. Mus.)

ALL England seemed alarmed at the growing
licentiousness of the Court of Charles II.
He cared more for the gratification of his pas-
sions than the good will of his people. Consequently he became the slave of any corrupt or
innocent woman who captivated his senses.
The money granted for raising a fleet against
the Dutch was used for the luxury and
depravity of his Court life. There was no
organisation in the navy, and the sailors
being discontented and dissatisfied because
their pay was not forthcoming, were refusing

o

to man the ships. Blood, Mason, and others had joined De Witt and De Ruyter, and it is believed that the boldness of the attack by the Dutch upon London was due to the influence of Blood, who, with De Witt, sailed up the Thames. Blood, knowing the feeling of the English sailors, attempted to persuade them to join the Dutch fleet, who, he said, "would pay them for their service." They then sailed into the Medway, burning the dock yard and all the shipping they could find in Chatham, and thus held London for some three weeks. Peace, however, was soon made, and the Triple Alliance agreed upon at Breda, in July, 1667. The following August, Thomas Holcroft, the brother of Maria (and Blood's brother-in-law), died, and we find him once more in the neighbourhood of Culcheth, but under an assumed name of Allen, not daring to reveal his identity. Maria and her two children were staying at Holcroft Hall, but Blood dare not accept hospitality under that roof again for fear of his capture. It is evident that his whereabouts was known at this time, for in the "State Papers," Domestic Series, Charles II., Vol. 189, No. 20, we read :—

"John Gryce, to Lord Arlington, 21st January, 1667-8. Hears that Captain Blood is gone for Lancashire, and resides about Warrington, by the name of Allen, or Groves. He will remain there till the end of February, when things will be more ready. Mr. Beech is suspected to be made an intelligencer of. The writer not thought deserving his livelihood . . . and a letter to the Duke of Ormond to go to Ireland, where he could discover any design on foot. Can send news without suspicion by Colonel Fitzjames, his landlord."

At this time there was a dispute about the Holcroft estate. Thomas Holcroft had died, having no surviving male issue, and one Richard Cavelvely began to put forth his claim to a certain portion of the estate. So violent was he in executing his supposed right, although his claim had been overruled by law for more than forty years, that he hired several loose and desperate characters from Wales, and came to the house of Hamlet Holcroft (a younger brother of Colonel Holcroft, who held and lived on the land to which Richard Cavelvely laid claim), and demanded possession. After a long dispute between the two gentlemen, pistols were pointed, which ended in Hamlet Holcroft being shot dead, and Richard Cavelvely, rightly or wrongly, coming into possession of the land. But of the main estate there were two claimants, Colonel

Blood, on behalf of his wife, who was the next in age of the children of Colonel Holcroft, and Charles, a younger brother. It was decided, however, that Charles, being the next male heir, he should hold the estate, and thus Blood's claim was overthrown. He once more returned to London, and practised as a physician, under the name of Ayliffe, and entered into the secret service of the Duke of Buckingham, whose duplicity and villainy were as great, if not as renowned as Blood's, who stood upon his honour when dealing with women, and put to shame the profligate Buckingham. In his employ he disguised himself as a courtier, a musician, a boatman, and an innkeeper, to carry out the many infamous plots and designs of that great Minister and attendant of His Majesty Charles II. It was thought that the attack upon the life of the Duke of Ormond was undertaken at the instigation of the Duke of Buckingham, who were both in favour at Court, but were open enemies. This, however, is not true, for Blood had a bitter hatred of Ormond, and he determined to avenge himself upon his old enemy. Though, at the same time, he may have thought that he would be doing my Lord Buckingham a good turn by ridding his rival's presence from the Court. In this exploit, he seems to have meditated hanging Ormond at Tyburn, but as the cat loves to torture and play with its victim, and often loses its prey in its play, so Blood, when his enemy was in his power, wished to torture him by delay of execution. He could have taken the life of the Duke on many occasions, but he was anxious to torture as well as to kill, and consequently lost his victim. Wherever Blood was he found able and willing accomplices in his daring exploits. He had on this occasion one Samuel Barrow and a Robert Tyldesley, old soldiers of the Parliamentary forces, who, like Blood, hated the Duke because of his treatment of them in Dublin ; also his own son, Thomas, who was just nineteen.

The Duke lived at Clarendon House, opposite St. James's Palace, and while returning home up St. James's Street, he was attacked, and dragged from his coach. It happened that while the Prince of Orange was visiting England the Duke was in attendance. It was on the sixth of December, 1670, that the attack was made. The Duke was always accompanied by six footmen, who walked on either side of the coach, and never was it known that he drove without this retinue, and to prevent the footmen from attempting to ride on the coach there were iron spikes projecting from the back. While the Duke was engaged with the young Prince of Orange at the dinner given in the city in his honour, Blood and his accomplices pursuaded the six footmen to a neighbouring inn, where, with assumed good fellowship, they made them helplessly intoxicated. With a handsome bribe to the landlord he settled for their safe keeping until morn. He then made his way to St. James's Street, and waited for the return of the Duke. It was decided that Blood and his son should enter the coach, and seize the Duke, while Robert Tyldesley secured the coachman. Samuel Barrow, who, by the way, was a powerful strong trooper, and over six feet, was to hold the horses, and receive the Duke upon his own. As the coach slowly dragged the sleeping Duke along, the three sprang from their hiding place. Robert Tyldesley mounted the seat of the driver, and held a pistol at his head. Blood and his son, one on each side, entered the coach, and dragged the sleeping Duke from his seat.

"How now, thou villain," said Blood. "I will shew thee no mercy, thou pious drunken hypocrite."

The Duke, recognising his voice, struggled, and shouted "Treason, treason," and then said, "What wilt thou now, thou blood-thirsty scoundrel? Wilt thou carry vengeance to the grave? Hast thou not been forgiven these many times for thy barefaced villainy, thou false knave?"

"Dost thou rail at me for villainy, and call me a false knave? Had I taken so much innocent blood as thou I would fain bury my head in the grave," replied Blood. "Thou art but fit for the gallows, and hanged thou shalt be this very night."

They mounted him upon Barrow's horse, and strapping him to the rider, they marched in a procession of triumph, Blood leading, and his son and Tyldesley on either side of the captured Duke.

"Hast thou no mercy for old age?" said the Duke, who was now just sixty.

"Mercy didst thou say? Oh! thou pious knave. When didst thou shew mercy to me and my troopers? Thou coverest thy villainy with a coat of religion, and prayest for mercy from him to whom thou shewedst no mercy. Nay, to the gallows thou shalt go," replied Blood.

Then turning to his son, he said, "Come, Thomas, let us go and make ready, and hasten ye with that pious hypocrite to Tyburn," he shouted to Barrow and Tyldesley as they rode off.

Meanwhile the coachman had driven to

Clarendon House, aroused the servants, and told them of the capture of the Duke. With all haste they ran along Piccadilly after them, passed Devonshire House, and on towards Knightsbridge, where they found the Duke lying helpless in the mud. Barrow had found a rough rider in the Duke, who had been determined to arouse attention. He kicked, shouted, and tossed about in mad fashion, until at last both riders fell to the ground. Tyldesley held his companion's horse, while they struggled together in the dark, until Barrow, hearing the shouts of the pursuing servants, released himself from the Duke, mounted his horse, and rode quickly away towards Tyburn to inform Blood of the misadventure. The Duke was completely exhausted, and could neither stand nor speak. He was bruised from head to foot, and with great difficulty they carried him to Clarendon

House, where he lay for some weeks. When King Charles heard of this malicious attempt on the life of his friend he was greatly disturbed, and issued a proclamation for the capture of Blood and a reward of £1,000. But neither Blood nor his accomplices were discovered. Young Ossory, the Duke's son, was so enraged at this assault, and suspecting Buckingham was the author of it, declared in the presence of the King that if his father came to a violent end he would pistol him though he stood behind the King's chair.

Part ii.

Chapter xx. The appointment of Sir Gilbert Talbot keeper of the Tower—Blood disguises himself as a clergyman —plans with Maria to steal the regalia—the plot fails—the introduction of his son with a view to marriage with Edward's daughter.

The Adventures

Part II

Chief Characters
COLONEL BLOOD AND MARIA.
MR. AND MRS. EDWARDS.
THOMAS BLOOD (Jun.) AND MISS
EDWARDS.

of Colonel Blood.

CHAPTER XX.

"Thanks, ye kind fates, for your last favour shown,
For stealing Blood, who lately stole the crown."

Elegy on Colonel Blood (Brit. Mus.)

UNTIL the year 1670 no one was allowed to
inspect the Crown jewels. Sir Gilbert
Talbot had been made Keeper of the Tower,
but so small was his salary, and so seldom
was it paid, that Sir Gilbert was granted
permission to admit the public on the
payment of a certain fee. By this means he
was able to appoint a keeper under him, who
accepted these fees in lieu of salary. Sir
Gilbert appointed a trusted and tried servant,
who with his family resided at the Tower.

Blood, for reasons which I am about to relate, determined to carry off the Crown jewels. In the Court of King Charles there had been some talk of selling the precious stones from the Crown jewels, as money from Parliament was not forthcoming to meet the heavy and lavish expenditure of the Court. Charles had already almost sold himself and his country to Louis of France. Secret negotiations had been going on, and £200,000 had been promised to Charles by him if he would become an ally with France to extend the Roman Catholic faith. In these negotiations he was backed up by Clifford and Arundel, who were both inclined to Romanism. Blood, though a desperado and an unprincipled man, was a Protestant in what he called his religious views, and he determined that the Crown should not rest upon the head of a Roman Catholic King.

And taking his wife into confidence, he dressed up as a clergyman, and with her visited the Tower. His first attempt was altogether unsuccessful, for he had thought it a simple plot to steal the Crown. He had planned that when the keeper had opened the door of the jewel house, and they had, for a few moments, admired the regalia, his wife should faint, and fall to the ground, assuming that the keeper would immediately go to her assistance, when he would hit him a blow with a club, and thus make him insensible. They then could carry off the Crown and jewels, hiding them under their cloaks and garments, and be well out of sight before the keeper regained consciousness. But the keeper did not, as assumed, bend down to assist the lady. He first locked all up, and called his wife to come to her assistance. After her feigned sickness had subsided the keeper's wife invited them to rest in the house, and behaved in a kindly and courteous manner, so that on leaving, the clergyman and his wife thanked them most profusely for their kindly act.

His first attempt thus thwarted, he determined upon another plan of greater duplicity, hoping by his friendliness he would be able to obtain the keys on some occasion when Mr. Edwards was not there, and thus secure the jewels. Accordingly he made special and frequent visits at all times of the day to the keeper's house, oftentimes taking presents, and declaring that he would ever remember their civility to his wife. On one occasion he took with him his son, whom he called his nephew, and who was to make love to the pretty daughter. The daughter was not there, having gone on a visit to her friends. Nothing daunted, he began to extol the good qualities of their daughter, and said : "This is my nephew. He hath a good fortune of some £300 a year, I brought him to see your gentle daughter. She hath a fair face, and the manners of a gentlewoman, and would make a good wife for him."

"Thou art indeed kind to suggest so happy an union. A handsome young man, with so handsome a fortune, is more than I could have desired for my gentle daughter," said Mrs. Edwards.

"If he wed thy daughter he will be a fortunate man," said Blood.

"And she would be a fortunate woman," replied Mrs. Edwards, as she looked at the young man. "But thou must bring the young man when she is returned from her visit."

Mrs. Edwards, who naturally thought that a handsome young man and three hundred a year was all that a girl could desire, had already made up her mind, and feeling quite generous, said, "Wilt thou and thy nephew sup with us to-night? My husband will shew thy nephew the Tower while I and the maid prepare the meal."

Blood assented only too gladly, that he might make a better survey of the situation, and form plans for his next visit, when he meant to carry off the jewels. He had thoroughly deceived the keeper and his wife. His religious dress, his pious expressions, his sober behaviour, had covered the plotting mind within, so that they never hesitated answering his questions, and shewing him whatever he desired. In the house there was a case of pistols, which he admired, and he expressed a wish to purchase them.

"But, sir, thou hast no use for such implements as these," said Edwards, "Thou hast to preach peace, and not war."

"Yea, thou hast rightly said my office is one to bring peace, and not war; but in these perilous days one must protect one's own body from violence. We know not what iniquitous plots may be laid against the Church. But it is not for myself that I would purchase the pistols. I was thinking of my neighbour, Lord——, who did me good service some short time ago, and that I could requite him for his kindness by presenting his Grace with so handsome a case of arms." But Edwards, not being willing to part with so valuable a set of pistols, Blood let the matter drop, lest he should arouse suspicion.

After supping, Blood and his son took their departure, expressing profuse thanks for so liberal a feast and so pleasant an evening, and agreeing with Mrs. Edwards upon a fitting day for the introduction of

his supposed nephew to the fair gentlewoman, they departed, he at the same time
suggesting that he should bring with him
two friends, who might be witnesses of the
wedding, and if the fair gentlewoman were
willing he would marry them there and then.

Mrs. Edwards replied "that she did not
think her daughter would object to so handsome and sober a young man."

Part ii.

Chapter xxi. Blood's early arrival at the Tower — his son's shyness while the crown jewels were being stolen —the arrival of Edwards' son — the thieves discovered—the escape and capture.

The Adventures

Chief Characters: COLONEL BLOOD, HIS SON.
HUNT AND PARROT.
MR. EDWARDS, HIS SON.
CAPTAIN BECKMAN.
MISS EDWARDS AND THE MAID.

CHAPTER XXI.

To carry out this second plot he selected his own son-in-law, for his daughter had married a young man, whose name was Hunt, and had come from the neighbourhood of Culcheth ; and one " Parrot," who had fought with Colonel Harrison at Warrington. On the day appointed he arrived with his accomplices early in the day. Mrs. Edwards and her daughter were not, however, ready to receive them. Blood therefore suggested that Edwards should show him and his companions the regalia, while his nephew

229

would remain below, and make his acquaintance with the gentle daughter. Blood's son assumed a strange shyness, and refused to enter the house, and stood at the door. This he did to keep watch while Blood and his accomplices did their work within. They had equipped themselves fully with arms, having hidden pistols and daggers under their cloaks, and rapier blades in their canes. No sooner had they entered the jewel house than the door was shut quickly, and a cloak thrown over Edwards, and gagged, while Blood proceeded to take the jewels. Edwards, perceiving that they were making an attempt to carry off the jewels, made as much noise as he could to arouse the household.

"If thou dost not stop thy kicking and blustering, I will put a bullet into thy head," said Hunt, who was holding him down while Blood and Parrot were hurriedly getting out the jewels. "Take that, thou foolish knave," as he stunned him with a wooden mallet, "thou wilt keep silence now," said Hunt.

Meanwhile, young Blood was still standing at the door, when the young lady, being dressed, and not liking to come down ere her mother was ready, sent the maid to see if the young gentleman was there. She found him standing alone outside.

"Wilt thou not come in?" said the maid. "My young mistress will be with thee presently."

"I will wait until my uncle returns," said young Blood, "he has gone with our friends to see the jewels."

"Art thou too simple to see thy young mistress alone? Indeed thou art a shy youth. I wager thou wilt not be so shy towards even. Come in, thou foolish lad, and I will fetch her to thee, and thou canst

231

make love to her to thy heart's content," she said. And away she went to tell her young mistress of the shy youth.

It was some time before the jewels could be obtained, and hid away under their cloaks. The sceptre was too large to carry without suspicion, so they began to file it in two ; so that Edwards regaining consciousness, and hearing the sound of a file, and feeling that silence was better than a mallet or a bullet, he kept so quiet that Hunt thought he was dead. They were filing away at the sceptre when a noise was heard outside. A son of Edwards had unexpectedly returned from Flanders, and at this moment he and his brother-in-law, Captain Beckman, suddenly arrived upon the scene.

Young Blood, still standing at the door, enquired "who they were, and with whom they wished to speak." The answer came as a terrible awakening to young Blood when he heard who they were. For a moment he stood speechless, and Edwards' son, perceiving he did not answer, said : "If thou hast any business with my father I will go and acquaint him." With these words he passed before him into the house. Hearing a noise, he went upstairs, and opening the door of the jewel house he saw the three robbers at work. The old man, hearing the door open, shouted, "Treason, murder, robbery." In a moment Hunt had given him a dagger wound in his breast. While young Edwards went to the rescue of his father the robbers escaped, leaving the sceptre, and carrying off the Crown, the orb, and some precious stones. The daughter, who had been anxiously waiting for her mother to go down to meet the young gentleman, heard the noise, and ran down, and took up the cry, shouting, "Treason. Murder. Stop the rogues ! "

Captain Beckman and young Edwards followed hard after them, but the conspirators fired at everyone who opposed them as they hurried away until they arrived at the drawbridge. They heard the cry after them, "Stop the rogues," "Treason," and as they ran along the Tower wharf they joined in the cry themselves, and so, being unsuspected, they got a good distance away. But Captain Beckman at last caught up to them, when Blood fired his last shot, and missed him. He was then seized after a desperate struggle, being encumbered with the Crown, which he was carrying under his cloak. "The devil take it," said Blood. "I have fought for a Crown, and lost it," as he at last, after a fierce and desperate fight, gave it up. Finally Parrot was captured, but his son and his son-in-law, being first to escape, got safely away. Horses were in waiting at St. Catherine's Gate, but only young Blood escaped. Hunt and two accomplices, who had been waiting to receive the stolen booty, were also captured. Parrot had been carrying the orb, and his breeches were full of the precious stones from the sceptre. During the fierce resistance on the part of the robbers many of the stones fell to the ground. The great pearl and a large diamond were afterwards found and restored. The Ballas ruby, a stone of great value, had been hid by Parrot, but when lodged in the White Tower it was afterwards found secreted in his breeches. Thus ended one of the most daring and impudent attempts of stealing the regalia recorded in history.

Part ii.

The Adventures

Chief Characters: KING CHARLES II. BUCKINGHAM.
ORMOND AND ARLINGTON.
SIR GILBERT TALBOT.
COLONEL BLOOD AND HIS CONFED-
ERATES.

CHAPTER XXII.

THE report of this terrible outrage upon the Crown jewels, and that Blood was the ringleader of the plot, spread quickly throughout the city. Sir Gilbert Talbot, who was informed by young Edwards, hurried to the Tower, to ascertain what really had happened. He then informed the King, who, being angry, commanded him to go forthwith, and take examination of Blood and his conspirators. The King was determined to punish them, but through the influence of Buckingham, the King's temper changed, and being curious to see the notorious Blood, he commanded him and the other prisoners to be brought to Whitehall to be examined by himself.

On either side the King sat Buckingham, Arlington, Ormond, and others of the Court; Sir Gilbert Talbot and young Edwards, with the prisoners, stood before them. In terms most severe and tremulous the King said:

"It is due to one who wishes thee well, and has prayed me to extend my clemency, that thou art here to-day. Thou knowest that thou art worthy only of the gallows, and this last deed of thy treacherous brain and bloody hand is beyond pardon. Wilt thou give us the names of those traitors, Protestants or Papists, who have paid thee to attempt this villainous deed?"

"His Majesty would not have me act the

traitor, and betray my compatriots?" answered Blood.

"If thou couldst save thy neck, and I were to extend my pardon, it were worth thy while," replied the King.

"His Majesty has misjudged me. My honour is of more value than my neck, and my pardon would be dearly bought if I sold my friends," replied Blood.

"Thou art a villain, a cutthroat, a robber, and dost thou talk of honour? Thou art but jesting. Tell me, therefore, thy instigators and accomplices, and I grant thee thy pardon," said the King.

"His Majesty can hang me, then, to-morrow at Tyburn, for I will never betray a friend, or defend myself to his injury," answered Blood.

"Thou talkest like a Puritan, and yet thou art a villain! Tell me, was it thee that attacked my friend, the Duke of Ormond, in St. James's Street?" asked the King.

"To that deed I confess the truth, and tell His Majesty that I intended to hang his Grace at Tyburn. It is to his Grace that His Majesy owns a subject such as I am. He dismissed me from the army, confiscated my property, and brought me to poverty," replied Blood.

"Thou dost accuse his Grace most falsely," replied the King, "for he is ever praying me to shew mercy, and extend my clemency to my subjects, and I warrant he will pray me to grant thee pardon."

"If pardon is not granted, I swear that His Majesty's and his Grace's neck will not be safe," answered Blood.

"What dost thou mean, thou insolent rogue?" asked the King.

"I wish His Majesty no evil; but if thou

takest my head there are a hundred com-patriots in the city who have sworn to avenge my death," replied Blood.

"Thou art a bold, impudent fellow, and thy speech is insolent," answered the King.

"But hear me further, for I would tell His Majesty," went on Blood, not heeding the King's remark, "that I have twice dropped my arm from taking His Majesty's life. Once when His Majesty was bathing at Battersea, and once when I saw him playing the fool with a lady, for whom I have the greatest honour and respect ; but the awe of Majesty checked my heart and my hand."

"Wouldst thou take the life of one who had done thee no ill ?" replied the King, who had already made up his mind to pardon him, and thus save his own neck.

"His Majesty makes me speak that which

all England is crying," answered Blood. "Thy foolish and corrupt life is doing ill to the nation, and killing the love of those who would be thy friends."

"Go, take the blatant fool hence," he said to Sir Gilbert Talbot. "I called the villain to Whitehall to judge him, and he has reprimanded me."

"Will His Majesty hear me further?" humbly asked Blood. "I would warn the King, and not insult him."

"Go on, thou hast the eloquence and the will of a Clarendon," replied the King.

"If His Majesty would spare the lives of my friends and myself it would save His Majesty and his Minister further harm, and His Majesty would make his enemies his friends," said Blood.

"Art thou craving pardon, then?" replied the King.

"Only that the pardon may spare His Majesty's neck," answered Blood.

"Take the fellow away," he said again to Sir Gilbert, and Blood and his accomplices were once more lodged in the White Tower.

In a few days the King sent Lord Arlington to the Duke of Ormond to say that he was granting Blood his pardon, and that he could not do so without his Grace's permission. He therefore asked him to pardon Blood for his attempt upon his life. The Duke answered in his formal politeness that "His Majesty's command was the only reason that could be given for granting his pardon. Yet as His Majesty chose to pardon the attempt to steal his Crown, he might easily consent that the attempt upon his life should be forgiven also." A messenger then was dispatched to the Tower with his pardon, and a letter informing him that his estate in Ireland would be returned to him, and £500 a year pension for the loss he had suffered. To Edwards and his son the only reward was £200 to the father, and £100 to the son, being grants from the Exchequer.

of Colonel Blood.

Part ii.

Chapter xxiii. Blood remains in London—enters into Society—presents a petition to King Charles II. for the Holcroft estate —enters into the secret service of the ministry—accused of plotting against Buckingham —his narrative—his death—exhumation and re-interment.

The Adventures

Chief Characters: BUCKINGHAM. SHAFTESBURY.
SALISBURY AND WHARTON.
KING CHARLES AND DANBY.
BLOOD, CHRISTIAN AND O'BRIEN.

of Colonel Blood.

CHAPTER XXIII.

"At last our famous hero, Colonel Blood,
Seeing his projects all will do no good,
And that success was still to him denied,
Fell sick with grief, broke his great heart, and died."

Elegy on Colonel Blood (Brit. Mus.)

BLOOD did not return to Ireland, but remained in London, and settled in Westminster. The promises of the King were not always kept. His £500 a year was not secure, and his presence in London would best demand its payment. Edwards and his son did not and could not receive their reward, so that they were glad to part with their right for half the sum.

Blood, being now pardoned, sought favour

in high circles, and went boldly into society. Evelyn, in his diary, says : " Dined with Mr. Treasurer's, where dined Monsieur de Gramont and several French noblemen, and one Blood, that bold impudent fellow, who had not long before attempted to steal the Imperial Crown out of the Tower itself."

In December of 1672 Charles Holcroft, who had held the Holcroft estate since the death of his brother Thomas, died without issue, and a second time Blood makes a claim to the estate. Having been admitted into court life he presents a petition to King Charles II., feeling confident that the King will interpose on his behalf. And in the Domestic Series, Charles II., Vol. 142, No. 19, we have a record of it.

To the King's most excellent Magtie.
The humble petition of Thomas Blood sheweth :

That yr petir, by ye late death of ye last heir male of John Holcroft, of Holcroft, of ye County of Lankester, Esq., in right of his wife, ye daughter of the said Holcroft, for ye recovery of which yr Petir hath a sute depending against some of ye family of the Holcrofts, who labour by all artifices to defraud yr Petir of his aforesaid just right, and finding their owne titell to be weake, have combined with one Richard Cavelvely to promote an old titell to his part of ye sd estate, which titell for this forty yeares hath beene overthrown at law, most of ye estate having belonged to ye Holcrofts and possessed above five hundred yeares, yet hath ye said Cavelvely been so vexatious, yt when his titell at law was rejected they laboured by violence to get footing in ye sd estate, and about six yeares ago they hyred severall obscure persons out of Wales, yt went

to ye house of a gentleman, one Hamlet
Holcroft, a relation of yr Petirs, and
with a pistoll killed him dead for not
giving them possession when they had
no legall prosis, nor officer to demand
it by, and some weekes since ye said
Richd. Cavelvely, being attached by
some of ye Sherife's Baylifs, according to
law concerning ye premises claimed by
yr Petitor, after they had him in custody ye sd Cavelvely catched up a
rapier, and killed one of ye said Baylifs
dead on ye place.

May it therefore please yr Magtie, out
of your Princely Grace, and for ye better
enabling yr Petir to serve yr Matie
(who is thereunto oblidged to his ut-
most power more than any person in ye
world) to confer upon yr Petr what
estate ye said Richd. Cavelvely layes
clame unto, or latly seized of ye aforesd
estate of John Holcroft and his heirs,
and consequently yr petr's, if yt upon

Cavelvely's tryall and conviction it shall
become forfeited to yr Magtie.

And yor Petr shall ever pray, etc.

The petition was not successful, and all
chance of ever inheriting the estate was cut
off by it passing into the family of Thomas
Tyldesley, a grandson of Sir Thomas Tyldesley, who had married Eleanor, a daughter
of Thomas Holcroft, Maria's brother, and
from that date all his and his wife's associa-
tions ceased for ever with the heirs of
Holcroft.

He was still a friend of the Duke of
Buckingham, and during the Cabal Ministry
he was in favour, and was of great service
to the Ministry.

In those days the feeling against the
Roman Catholics was growing stronger, as
they were growing more in favour at Court.
But the power which they had with the

R

King, and the secret alliance with Louis and Charles, was at last broken. It was quietly done by an opposite alliance, namely, by the marriage of Mary, daughter of the Duke of York, with the Prince of Orange, the result of which was the greatest blessing to England, and saved it from another conflict between the King and his people.

The King had been subsidised by Louis, to keep England from helping the Dutch, and this he did by twice proroguing Parliament. Even his best friends protested against this unwarrantable action, and such gross intrigue with France. Lords Shaftesbury, Salisbury, Wharton, and Buckingham, who protested, were imprisoned in the Tower for more than a year, and the Earl of Danby became Prime Minister. But through the able and secret service of Blood it was discovered that he also was in connivance with

of Colonel Blood.

Louis of France. Through Blood a letter was produced, in which Danby craved for money from the French King, and he was condemned. This released his friend Buckingham and the others from the Tower. To save Danby's head, however, Charles dissolved Parliament. But the new Parliament was as much against Danby as the previous one, and proceeded to take action against him, and on March 6th he was sent to the Tower. Blood himself was most bitter against the influence of the Roman Catholics, and though not himself implicated in the extraordinary plot which had been concocted, and revealed by Titus Oates; yet when the whole country was filled with fear at the intrigue of the Papists, and there being much liberty of the Press, he published a narrative of a Romish plot, in which he himself was to be destroyed. This narrative was his last attempt at intrigue and plot. The changes of affairs in Parliament both indicted him and saved him from a felon's death. Shaftesbury and the other three Lords who had been released from the Tower, were again coming into power. The country was so excited and fierce at the discovery of so much intrigue by the revelation of the Titus Oates plot, that many Peers and Jesuits were imprisoned, convicted and executed, and any persons connected with the many narratives of the plots which were written at this time were seized and imprisoned.

The passing of the Habeas Corpus Act on May 29th, 1679, which was the second Act only in importance to the Magna Charta, secured the liberty of the subjects. Kings and Queens aforetime had, at their will and caprice, and without restraint, sent their enemies, or friends if they wished to be rid of them for a time, to the damp and unwholesome prisons. Mary Queen of Scots had been confined for nineteen years, and when led to the scaffold was crippled with rheumatism through the dampness of the dungeon, and bowed with premature old age by the solitary confinement. Sir Walter Raleigh was imprisoned for twelve years, and Archbishop Laud for four years, in damp and unwholesome solitary cells, and were brought forth, ruined in health and body. But the Habeas Corpus Act prevented even a monarch from keeping the meanest subject in prison beyond a certain length of time without a proper trial. This Act saved Blood's life, though not for long. He was accused, with two Papists, named Edward Christian and Arthur O'Brien, and indicted in the King's Bench, for a plot against his friend the Duke of Buckingham, which they gathered from the narrative of the plot which he had published. This was a false charge, for though he and the Duke were unprincipled and designing rogues, this charge could not be laid against Blood. But it was proved from the narrative that he had been associated with these men, and found guilty. He found bail for £10,000, and was released. This was in June, 1680. Though he had been associated with these men, it was only to find out further plots and schemes which he intended to make known to the Government, and to be falsely accused at the last so preyed upon his mind and affected his health that he died in a state of lethargy, on August 24th, 1680.

A few days after he was buried, a report began to be spread that the real Colonel Blood was not dead. So remarkable had been his career that people had said that "he could not die." He had gone through more encounters, had done more violent deeds, had shed more innocent blood than any adventurer of his day. The character of his exploits was so glaringly bold and his powers of impersonation so great, and his sudden exit from the scene of crime so miraculous, that the superstitious could not believe that it was his body which had been buried. To clear the air of so alarming a report the Coroner summoned a jury, had his body raised, and called upon his relatives to identify the remains. The only proof that the now decaying body was that of the notorious Colonel Blood was the abnormal size of his thumbs. Thus identified, his body was again interred, and left to go the way of all flesh in Tothills Fields, September, 1680.

The Adventures of Colonel Blood.

Thus died the notorious Thomas Blood, whose deeds of violence, and whose escapes from justice were beyond belief, if they had not been true. Thus truth is stranger than fiction.

The Epitaph.

HERE lies the Man who boldly hath run through
More Villanies than ever ENGLAND knew
And nere to any friend he had was true
Here let him then by all unpittied lye
And let's Rejoyce his time was come to Dye.

Finis.

Appendix.

APPENDIX.

CULCHETH OR KILCHETH (*from "Camden's Britannia,"* 1695). — After Chatmoss we see Holcrofte, which both gave seat and name to the famous family of Holcrofts, formerly enriched by marriage with the coheir of Culchit, for that place stands hard by; which Gilbert de Culchit held in See of Almarick Butler, as Almarick did of the Earl de Ferraries in Henry the Third's time, whose eldest daughter and heir being married to Richard, the son of Hugh de Hinley, he took the name of Culchit, as Thomas, his brother, who married the second daughter, was called from the estate, Holcrofte; the other for the same reason, Peasfurlong, and the fourth, de Riseley. Now I note this, that the reader may see that our ancestors as they were grave and settled in, so in rejecting old and taking new names from their possessions, were light and changeable. Some famous families have the same name to this very day, as Aston of Aston, Atherton of Atherton, Tillesley of Tillesley, Standish of Standish, Worthington of Worthington, Troutbeack of Troutbeack.

Note i.—A most interesting discovery was made on the 26th of May, 1851, which lends interest and accuracy to the story, and which I trust will interest the reader. In pulling down an old house near the "Plough" Inn, in Houghton Winwick, two bundles of papers were found. They were thrust into the roof of the house as if for concealment or safe custody, just above the plaster and below the thatch. One bundle was folded up and the other was tied round with a cord. The house was once the residence of Thomas Sargeant, the constable of Houghton, whose name is more than once mentioned in the papers. Some of the papers are torn, being minus a piece here and there, and so are hard to decipher. They are in the Warrington Museum, and the writer has had the privilege of getting the substance of those papers relating to the characters of the narrative and to Culcheth, and gives them as being items of especial value. Most of them refer to the earlier siege of Warrington and the commencement of the Civil Wars :—

Petition from the inhabitants of Southworth-with-Croft to Wm. Alcock and Captain Coney, complaining that Captain Holcroft had favoured the Township of Culcheth by imposing on Southworth-with-Croft an unfair proportion of men. Dated 6th January, 1642.

Precept. Richard Astley to the constables of Culcheth, Southworth-with-Croft, Middleton and Arbury, dated 9th March, 1642, under the authority of a warrant from the Earl of Derby, ordering an assessment on Culcheth, to raise £43 10s. od., and Southworth-with-Croft, Middleton and Arbury, £21 15s. od.

Note (private) intimating that Lord Mollineux's precept to the Township of Culcheth demanded 30 bushels of oats, 180 stone of hay, and £4 10s. od. in money.

The following is the facsimile of the warrant :—

These are to will and require and immediately to charge and command you that, immediately upon receipt hereof you summon and require all men and others of ability with your townes, to come and appear before us at Winwick upon Fryday next, being the 26th of May........................to lende and contribute money............................of Parliament............if they will avoyd............ of their estats and securinge theire persons ....p'voyed and...............able men furnished withe spads and mattocks and 3 day's p'vic of...............for such service for the..................as shall be appointed them ; and further ye shall gather in and p'voyd ....victuals for p'vicion of our armes, and bringe it and the............in to-morrow morning to Bewsey Hall, as you will answer the contrary at your uttermost p'ill. Given under our hands this 24th day of May, 1643. T. Stanley, Richard Holland, Peter Edgerton, and John Houlcrofte.

To the Constables of Sothworth-with-Croft.

Precept signed by Stanley, Egerton and Holcroft, dated 11th July, 1643, and addressed to the Constable of Southworth - with - Croft ordering an apportionment in the township for raising £10 in pursuance of an order from the Lieutenant of the County at a Meeting at Rochdale.

Warrant from Thomas Holcroft to the Constables of Houghton, date 29th May, 1646, to bring in four persons therein named, to provide a soldier, or serve in person.

(Warrington Museum.)

Note ii.—Truth is the daughter of time, and the fact recorded of the wounded man falling from the steeple received a singular confirmation in 1854, when in digging a grave near to the steeple a skeleton was found with an iron bullet embedded in its thigh bone.—(Beaumont.)

Note iii.— Carlyle (in " Cromwell's Letters," Vol. I., 360) thus notices this battle :—" The Duke of Hamilton, at the head of a large army, having entered England with the intention of restoring the King, was encountered by Cromwell near Preston, on the 17th of August, and the battle, a sort of running fight, in which the Duke was always worsted, continued for three days. His army made its last stand at Red Bank, near Winwick, where, according to Sir James Turner (Dugald Dalgetty, as Carlyle persists in calling him), they were commanded by a little spark in a blue bonnet, who performed the part of an excellent commander, and was killed on the spot." " Does anyone," asks Carlyle, continuing the story, " know this little spark in the blue bonnet? No one. His very mother has long ceased to weep for him now. Let him have burial and a passing sigh from us." The question which Carlyle, in his moralising, thus asks, but does not answer, we believe we are able to answer for him, and to "give the little spark in the blue bonnet" the name of Major John Cholmley, who is recorded to have been buried in the chancel of Winwick Church on the 3rd of September, 1648, and who, of all who fell, is the only person mentioned to have been buried after the battle. The only relics of the battle are a large handsome spur, a few cannon balls, and two coins (kept in the Warrington Museum), and some camp kettles, which are preserved in Winwick. At a much later period (15th September, 1665), Roger Lowe, the diarist, says he found a sadder memorial of the battle,—a head which had ever since remained unburied,—and that he took it and buried it.—(Beaumont.)

Note iv.—During this rest, Cromwell saw the Winwick Grammar School, where John Howe, who became his most faithful secretary and spiritual adviser, was educated. Whether on this occasion he met Howe in Winwick it is impossible to say, for he was about entering upon his University career at the time. From Winwick he went to Cambridge, but migrated to Oxford, where he became a fellow and Chaplain of Magdalen College, Oxford, and was ordained in Winwick Church in 1652 by the celebrated Herle, after the Presbyterian form. In 1644 an Ordinance of Parliament had passed, empowering Herle and others to ordain ministers in Lancashire, and he continued in the same office when Presbyterianism was established. Herle, who took the principal part in his ordination, was probably assisted by the ministers of the several chapels in his large parish; and therefore we may be assured that William Leigh, who married both Colonel Blood and Thomas Holcroft at Newchurch, which was a chapelry of Winwick, took part in it; for Howe used to say, "there were few men whose ordination had been so truly primitive as his, having been devoted to his work by a primitive Bishop and his officiating presbytery."

Baxter called John Howe "a very judicious godly man, of no faction, but of Catholic healing principles." He certainly was a man with a most Catholic spirit for a Presbyterian, as he showed when Fuller, an Episcopalian and a staunch Royalist, appealed to him. Fuller, who had been appointed to the Rectory of Waltham, having to satisfy the Committee of "Tryers" before he could enter upon it, applied to Howe. "You see," he said, "I am a somewhat corpulent man, and I am to go through a very straight passage. I beg you to give me a shove

and help me through." And Howe gave
him such advice as enabled him to satisfy his
examiners without crossing his own conscience.
It is recorded of Howe, and the reader will
pardon me for inserting it here, that he asked so
many favours of Cromwell for others, that Cromwell once said to him, "I wonder when the time
will come that you will ask something for your-
self?" To which he replied, "My Lord, my
turn is always come when I can serve another."
—*Beaumont's History of Winwick.*

Note v.—William Leigh was one of the Cur-
ates of Winwick under the learned Charles
Herle. When the Lancashire Provincial classes
were established, Charles Herle is set down as
the Minister at Winwick, and William Leigh
the Minister at Newchurch.

Note vi.—Colonel Lilburne's letter to Colonel
Birch, Governor of Liverpool, after the battle :—

"Wigan, 15th Aug., 1651.
"Honoured Sir,
"The Lord hath pleased, this day, to
appear for us, in the totall rout and overthrow
of the Lord of Derby and his forces, which was
increased to about 15,00. He himself, though
wounded, escaped, though narrowly. I would
only entreat you to send out what horse you
have, or can get, to ride up and down the country to gather up stragglers. I cannot enlarge
myself at present, but I entreat you to accept of

this from him that desires to expresse himself. Your ammunition is come safe. The Lord of Derby I heare is fled towards Bolton, but his sumptures and tresure are here. We intended for Manchester this night, and had hope to take my Lord Generall's regiment of foot, and to have had five hundred men in readinesse to joyne with them. The Lord Witherington cannot live long. Colonels Boynton and Tyldesley are slaine, and others very considerable. I have divers collonels prisoners.

"Your very humble servant,

"Robert Lilburne.

"For my honoured friend Col. Birch, governor of Liverpool, these haste."

Col. Birch's letter to Mr. Speaker :—

Liverpool, August 26th, 1651.
"Sir,

"It hath pleased the Lord, yesterday, to give an utter overthrow by Col. Lilburne's regiment of horse to the Earl of Derbie, who was raising men here in this county for the Scot's King. The Earl, at his coming over from the Isle of Man, brought but 300 men, whereof 60 were horse; but landing about the middle of the shire, when the Scot's army were passing out of it, he had the better opportunity, by our destractions, to march up to Warrington to them, and there he had the assistance of Major General Massey, with a regiment of horse to countenance his proceedings, while he gathered more to him;

who afterwards leaving him when the Earle's forces were reputed considerable, to carry on the worke, and there being none in this county left competent to make opposition, but all marched out with the army. I sent both to my Lord Generall and Major Generalls to acquaint them with it, whereupon Col. Lilburne came very opportunely; yet the enemy being stronger in foot, and seeing himself betwixt two rivers, he was not to be attempted by horse only, and all that could be afforded in assistance were two foot companies from Chester, one of my regiments, left about Manchester, not being ready as the rest to march out, and what musketeers I horsed from hand, with some few country men; but since my Lord Generall's owne regiment of foot being sent up, and within one day's march, the enemy attempted towards the Scot's army, and being pursued by Col. Lilburne's regiment, and the small addition before named, without the conjunction of my Lord Generall's regiment, it pleased God to give them an absolute overthrow, as the enclosed from Col. Lilburne intimates. The number of the prisoners and the slaine, with their qualifications, I cannot yet give further account of, but I hope the successe prevents all designs in these parts. I must excuse for this distracted letter,

"And ever am, Sir, your most reall and humble servant,   "Thomas Birche.

"For the Right Honourable William Lenthal, Esq., Speaker of the Parliament of the Commonwealth of England, at Westminster, these presents."

Note vii.—Buried Aug. 27th, 1651. My Lord Witherington de Northumberland, Collnell Boyneton de Yorkshire, Collnell Trolope, Governor of Newark.—Wigan Parish Registers.

Note viii.—As late as 1874 relics of the skirmish were found. On widening the road leading from Culcheth to Leigh, near the Raven Inn, a mound in an adjoining field was removed, in which were found bones and rusted weapons. The sign of the Raven is that of a Raven with drawn sword in its claw, standing on the dead body of a soldier.

Note ix.—In Ireland they (the Anabaptists) were grown so high that the soldiers were many of them re-baptised as the way to preferment, and those that opposed, crushed with much uncharitable fierceness. To suppress these he sent hither his son, Henry Cromwell, who so discountenanced the Anabaptists, as yet to deal civilly by them, repressing their insolencies, but not abusing them, or dealing hardly with them.—(Rel. Baxterianae.)

Note x.—The Act of Uniformity, passed on May 19th, 1662, enacted that not only every Clergyman, but every Fellow of a College, or Schoolmaster, should accept everything contained in the Book of Common Prayer.

Note xi.—The meeting house still stands, surrounded by its little graveyard, wherein are the remains of the Founder, and is used for public worship. It is about five miles from Warrington and Leigh. There is an old endowment of about £50 left by the Risleys and others. The Ministers in turn fell from Orthodoxy to what was called Arminianism, and from Arminianism to Socinianism, and the Incumbency was held by that school of thought for some time. Several gentlemen, including the Rector of Winwick, took action in 1839 against the Unitarians, and a favourable decision was obtained. The first trust deed stated that the parties in possession should be Presbyterians, and hold the doctrinal articles of the Church of England, but a new trust deed was drawn up, in which the Minister is to be a bona-fide English Presbyterian.

Note xii.—The five mile act forbade any Minister to teach in Schools, to come within five miles of any Corporate town or Parliament borough who had not subscribed to the Act of Uniformity, or who would not swear to a doctrine of passive obedience, and pledge himself that he would not at any time endeavour any alteration in Government of Church or State.

Note xiii.—James Sharp, a Presbyterian minister, who was sent to London to plead the cause of the Presbyterians, betrayed their cause, and returned Archbishop of St. Andrews.

Note xiv.—The One Mile Act forbade any recusant minister to reside within twenty miles of his own parish, or within three miles of a royal borough.

Appendix

Note xv.—John Middleton, a rough soldier of fortune, who had risen entirely from the ranks, was created an Earl, and made Royal Commissioner of Scotland. A cruel, hardhearted, and, Burnet says, a drunken man.

Note xvi.—Lauderdale, the Secretary of State for Scotland, also a Presbyterian, and renegade, imprisoned and persecuted the Covenanters.

www.ingramcontent.com/pod-product-compliance
Lightning Source LLC
Chambersburg PA
CBHW022313280626
47169CB00020BB/2913